On the Wapiti Range

When the hunting party in search of a trophy wapiti arrives on Lee Trent's Green River preserve, his first inclination is to show them the road out. Arrogant and demanding, they have brought too much potential trouble and too many guns to his peaceful realm. If that weren't enough, they are also holding prisoner a beautiful madwoman in a windowless wagon.

The elk hunters' presence threatens to bring Lee into conflict with the Cheyenne Indians, his neighbours and friends and disaster follows when the hunt becomes a slaughter. Now Lee must handle the invaders by himself if he is to recover his mountain domain.

On the Wapiti Range

Owen G. Irons

A Black Horse Western

ROBERT HALE · LONDON

ISBN-10: 0-7090-7979-6
ISBN-13: 978-0-7090-7979-8

Robert Hale Limited
Clerkenwell House
Clerkenwell Green
London EC1R 0HT

Typeset by
Derek Doyle & Associates, Shaw Heath
Printed and bound in Great Britain by
Antony Rowe Limited, Wiltshire

ONE

Calvin Manassas stepped out into the bright sunlight from his roughly built cabin. He had heard something approaching. The sound was unusual and so, respecting all of the instincts of caution, he carried his hard-used but meticulously maintained Winchester repeating rifle in his right hand.

The morning was clear except for a few horse-tail banners of thin cloud sketched against the high sky of Wyoming. The Rocky Mountains to the east were stark and clear, maintaining a burst of sunrise color in the gaps. The day was not old.

The air was clean and cold in early fall. The breeze was light, but it toyed with the concept of oncoming winter. The high peaks, all of 14,000 feet high, were capped with eternal snow. Long, unfurled pennants of white ran down their dark slopes until they met the timber-line where the

5

tall blue spruce and jack pines spread in endless depths.

The sounds continued to approach. Now Cal could hear well enough to determine that there were wagons on the trail leading to his small homestead. One of them had an ungreased axle rasping and whining with each revolution. With his free hand Calvin shaded his eyes and peered southward. He was a narrow man, his gray-shot, home-cut hair sticking up in spikes. He had not shaved yet and the white of many winters showed in the whiskers along his narrow cheeks and jutting jawline.

His yellow hound, Jack, had emerged yawning from his sleeping place under the house. He scratched his ear a few times and then began to bark enthusiastically as the train of wagons drew into view, emerging from the creek bottom pines.

Calvin's few cattle – he had thirty-four in all – scattered as the strangers interrupted their morning cud chewing. Calvin reached inside the cabin, removed his flop hat from its peg and planted it on his head. He at first believed that a lost group of settlers had missed the Green River ferry crossing. Then he had hopefully considered that it was his old friend, Frank D'Arcy, the whiskey peddler and drummer, arrived early this year. It was neither.

It was the strangest entourage Calvin Manassas

had ever encountered in his years on the Wyoming basin. He squinted into the early sunlight, making out: first, two men in black uniforms with brass buttons on their coats wearing shiny helmets, secondly a four-wagon train, each wagon driven by other men in uniform, thirdly a party of seven men, two of them in dude clothing of a cut he had never seen before. One of the two men who now took the lead sported a gray upturned, waxed mustache that seemed to cover half of his face. The other was American, but he sat his big horse in eastern fashion. Calvin removed his hat, scratched his head and stepped out to meet the arriving party.

The wagons held back and two of the men, flanked by the guards in polished helmets, approached the cabin. No one swung down from his horse or smiled.

'Howdy,' was all Calvin could think to say.

The two men sitting in front of the group walked their horses a little closer. The stallion the obviously Eastern man rode was black as obsidian, deeply muscled and heavy in the chest. The other man, the one with the vast mustache, a foreigner of some sort, sat a white horse with a twitchy attitude about it. The man on the black horse wore a buckskin jacket, but there was what seemed to be lace at the cuffs of his shirt. Calvin frowned.

'My name is Darby Pierce,' the American man said. He was thick in the chest, thick in the face. He waited as if that name was supposed to mean something to Calvin.

'Happy to meet you, Mr Pierce. Would you and your friends care for some coffee? I was about to boil some up. The trough is that way,' he said with a jerk of his head, 'if your horses are thirsty.'

'We are seeking information,' Pierce said stiffly. His accent, Calvin thought, was Bostonian. At least from that part of the East.

'Fine,' Calvin said. 'Be happy to help.' Jack the hound had gone off to sniff at each horse in turn. The tall white stallion kicked at him and the man with the huge mustache was jostled in his saddle.

'Jack, you be good. Get home!' Calvin said and the dog obligingly slunk back toward the sagging front porch to lie down on his belly and soak in the morning sun rays.

The American swung down and the portly European with the mustache followed after waiting for one of the helmeted guards to hold his horse's bridle for him. These two tramped across the dusty stretch of yard to Calvin's cabin. Neither of them smiled. Calvin thrust his hand out and the Easterner shook it briefly with a hand that, though uncallused, was strong in its grip. The European man only looked at Cal's hand and refused to raise his own. Calvin smiled inwardly.

8

'A man welcoming you into his own house expects some civility,' he said. The puffy European stiffened. Darby Pierce intervened quickly.

'The baron is not used to Western ways,' he said. 'Please, may we go inside?'

'Certainly,' Cal Manassas agreed, gesturing to the open door. He turned his head and spat. Jack, the yellow hound, he reflected had better manners than this stranger. In the far places, however, a man was remiss if he didn't offer guests food or drink as they required, and after letting the two men enter his cabin before him, he followed, Jack at his heels.

The baron stood looking around the one-room shack, his eyelids drooping. Darby Pierce sank onto a puncheon chair and smiled ineffectively at the Wyoming rancher. Calvin said, 'I'll start some coffee, men, and you can tell me what it is that brings you out all this way.'

It was left to Darby Pierce to speak as Calvin prodded the wood in his iron stove to life, filled the gallon coffee pot with water and roughly measured fresh ground coffee.

'As you may have gathered,' Darby Pierce said, removing his hat and placing it on the table – crown down, another indication that he was not a Western man. Out in the wilds there was a custom, not really a superstition, of removing your hat so that it was open to prevent your luck from running out, 'This is a hunting expedition.'

The Easterner went on. 'My brothers and I own a shipping company in Baltimore and the baron and his friends have expressed a desire to visit our wild West and get in some hunting while here. You may know Baron Stromberg by name. . . .'

'No, sir,' Calvin said, scratching at his disordered thicket of gray hair. 'The only baron I ever did hear of was this man called Munchausen.' The baron stiffened. Calvin couldn't guess how much English the man understood, but he supposed he had somehow insulted the nobleman.

'Baron Stromberg,' Pierce said hastily, 'is from Prussia, and I assure you, a member of a very successful family of traders.'

'That's fine,' the old mountain man said, pouring the boiled coffee into three tin cups using a rag as a hot pad. He poured a tablespoon of cold water into each to cause the grounds to drop, then served the men. Stromberg had continued to stand; now with a tight-lipped glance at the roughly made wooden chair, he seated himself. 'What can I do for you gents?' Calvin asked.

The baron continued to watch Calvin from beneath heavy eyelids as if he were bargaining with some untrustworthy barbarian prince. Pierce continued although Calvin Manassas seemed to pay more attention to Jack, the yellow hound, than to him. He petted the dog's wide skull and scratched it under the chin, causing Jack's leg to twitch in response.

Pierce colored slightly, but he continued. 'The baron and his friends have been hunting in the West for three months now. He has taken his share of buffalo, three mountain lions, one moose, more than twenty mule deer, five or six mountain sheep, a couple of badgers and hundreds of grouse, one black bear, three grizzlies, at least twenty pronghorn antelope. . . .'

'Sounds like he's pretty well cleaned us out,' Calvin said laconically. He tilted back in his chair and sipped at his strong gritty coffee. Outside the men loitered around the wagons or watered their horses. A few of them had broken out pipes and were smoking at their leisure. A cook had begun to cook something savory on a portable black iron stove.

Pierce smiled and then went on with a glance at the baron. He looked to Calvin like a new employee trying to please his boss, which, he supposed Darby Pierce was in a way if he was trying to cement a deal between a major European import-export enterprise and his own Baltimore shipping line.

'The wapiti,' the Prussian said between clenched teeth. He had not even reached for his coffee cup.

Pierce continued, 'Before returning to Europe the baron wishes to collect one more trophy, a wapiti.'

'Elk,' the baron said in the same manner.

'I'm sure Mr Manassas knows what a wapiti is,' Pierce said, trying for friendliness. Still there was a glimmer of anxiety in the back of his eyes as if he feared offending the baron, a potentially powerful trading partner.

'Ain't no wapiti roaming this low just yet,' Manassas said. He had found a corncob pipe and without fresh tobacco, he fired up the cold tarry dottle that remained in it. 'By 'low', I mean in the basin. To you three, four thousand feet might not seem that low, but it is for the big elk herds. Soon as the first snow begins to fall in the high reaches, they'll begin to drift down, but that'll be a month at least.'

'Is he saying he cannot help us?' the baron demanded and now Calvin had an idea just how much English Stromberg did speak. Enough.

'I didn't say that, exactly,' Calvin replied, holding up one hand as he strained to get his pipe going. 'I said they don't normally come this low this time of year. There's a herd of maybe two hundred wapiti that range not far from here, but they're on the Lee Trent parcel.' Calvin shook his head, blowing out a stream of acrid smoke. 'I can't speak for Lee Trent. I don't know if he'd want any truck with you.'

'Truck!' the Prussian sputtered.

'I don't know if he'd agree to have you on his parcel, that is,' Calvin replied. The dog got up and went out onto the porch to watch the convoy of visitors.

'There's money in it for him,' Pierce insisted.

'For you as well,' the baron persisted. 'I wish to obtain the trophy.'

'I can speak to Lee Trent,' Calvin said. Shaking his head, he added, 'But I don't know how he'd feel about trophy hunting on his parcel.'

'You keep calling it a *parcel*,' the man from Baltimore said, sipping at his own coffee. 'What do you mean by that? I understand the term loosely, of course, but what exactly does that mean out here? How much land does he own?'

Calvin rubbed the back of his hand against his snowy whiskers. It took him a minute to respond. 'Well, sir, it's like this: Lee Trent don't own any land out here. He has a "parcel" of about two hundred square miles.'

'If he doesn't own it . . .' the baron said growing more deliberate. Calvin lifted a broken, callused hand.

'Things are different out here, sir. Here is what Lee's parcel means: a long time ago Lee did a great favor for the Green River Cheyenne band.

What it was, even I don't know. Lee don't like to talk about it too much.

'You have to understand, as few as five years ago there was still warfare between the Cheyenne and the whites. Well, even now it wouldn't take much to set that tinderbox up in flames. Anyway,' Calvin said, now content since his pipe had begun to draw well, 'Lee did the Cheyenne this great favor. The Cheyenne are a generous people. When they asked Lee Trent what he wanted in return – a hundred ponies! Wives! Lee told them that he wanted to be free to live on the land where warfare would never come.'

'And they gave him . . .' Pierce began, now caught up in the story.

'They *gave* him nothing, sir. Among the Cheyenne land is not something that can be owned, bought or traded. They gave Lee his "parcel", meaning that no Cheyenne can come upon his land to hunt or trap without his permission, that the fur, the game, the timber is his and no man can encroach upon it.'

'His own fiefdom,' Pierce said. Calvin smiled.

'No, sir – if I understand the word – Lee is free to live on it without interference, without fear of betrayal. That is the Cheyenne law. He has no fences, he has no lumber camps or mines. He lives as he wishes in complete peace.

'So!' Calvin told them, 'I am not sure if he

would allow anyone to hunt the land. Not for trophies,' Calvin said with a small shake of his head.

'Surely he hunts there!' the baron said, rising an inch or two.

' 'Course,' Calvin answered evenly, 'but a man like Lee Trent uses what he kills as an Indian would. The hide of an elk or a buffalo makes for moccasins and a winter coat, blankets and such. The meat is quartered and smoked or left out in the winter to last frozen – unless the timber-wolves find it. He uses the elkhorn for the buttons on his jacket. The hoofs, boiled down, become mighty good glue . . . Lee doesn't waste any more of the animal than an Indian does. Five or six a year can see him through for meat.'

'Surely,' Darby Pierce said, leaning forward intently, 'he must need more.' His hand waved toward the stove, 'Coffee, flour, cornmeal, sugar, beans, lard, salt!'

'I will give him five hundred dollars for the wapiti,' the baron said. 'A span of five to six feet on the antlers. Five hundred gold American dollars. Surely the man is not stupid! He must have needs he wishes to satisfy.'

Calvin was silent, turning his cup on the table. 'I couldn't say. I can't speak for another man.'

'Will you talk to him!' Pierce pleaded. 'This is important to the baron. Fifty dollars just to speak to him! Fifty more if you convince the man,' he said, without a glance at the baron. 'Baron Stromberg must have his trophy collection complete. It is essential.'

'I can't see why it's essential,' Calvin said, speaking the word as if it were sour. He thought of the oncoming winter and the use he could have for fifty dollars. He shrugged, 'I'll talk to Lee Trent, though I can promise nothing.'

After the meeting Calvin was left with many questions. He went out alone, his dog beside him, to think matters over. The hunting party had made itself at home in his yard. The cook's fire continued to burn and the scent of venison was heavy in the air. That and onions and a variety of spices unfamiliar to Calvin. An assortment of men had exited the wagons, drawn up in a half circle near Calvin's stone well. His few cattle had moved away in a loose bunch, made nervous by the gathering.

Deciding that he wished to have a closer look at the hunting party, he walked unremarked among the guards, hunters and wagons. One of the wagons had its tailgate dropped and a man was working there. Calvin started that way and then halted abruptly as he got a look at what the wagon contained.

Within the wagon where the man with a scraping tool worked was a pile of bones, antlers and whole skeletons. He saw bear paws hanging from hooks placed along the wagon's side and a stack of furs pushed further into the corner. The taxidermist, for that was what he proved to be, glanced up at Calvin and then bent to his work again.

'The baron has had some luck,' Darby Pierce said, appearing at Calvin's side. The man from Baltimore was taller than Calvin had first thought and his face was broad and hard, sheltering pale blue eyes. 'Those specimens will raise some eyebrows in Europe.'

'They'd raise some out here,' Calvin said trying to keep his tone neutral. These men had no use for these animals. They had killed them without need and done it profligately.

'Let me show you something that might interest you,' Pierce said. He was trying to be affable, it seemed, but he must have read Calvin's eyes for the smile in his eyes died away. Shrugging, Calvin followed the man to a second wagon. This one was constructed entirely of wood with a hinged stairway leading to a heavy wooden door, something like a gypsy caravan's wagon, Calvin thought. He followed Pierce up the stairs and into the wagon's interior.

Pierce slid a shutter wide and light streamed in to glint on the gleaming cargo the wagon held. Calvin whistled softly despite himself. Every inch of one wall was hung with magnificent hunting arms. Long barreled, short barreled, octagon and round. The receivers were embossed and inlaid with gold and silver depictions of game. The stocks were of gleaming black oak or bird's eye maple, polished to furniture brightness.

'Never seen nothing like these,' Calvin said. Darby Pierce had removed a large-bore rifle from its hook and showed it Calvin. Pheasants in gold soared skyward from a silver meadow and stags, their heads held high, watched in surprise.

'It's Belgian-made of course,' Pierce said. Why *of course*, Calvin Manassas didn't understand, but it was a beautiful piece of workmanship, the kind of weapon that should have been displayed in a museum not trundled around the West in this wagon.

'Remarkable,' Calvin said, handing the rifle back. 'What caliber?'

'This is a .45-.90. Quite suitable for anything smaller than an elephant.'

'I should guess. Where do you find the ammunition for such a piece?' Calvin wondered.

'Oh, that,' Pierce said, replacing the rifle. 'We have our own reloader with us. A man named Glass. He keeps a ready stock of powder and lead, bullet molds and casings available.'

'The baron doesn't want for much, it seems,' Calvin said. He himself carried a Colt revolver and a Winchester .44-.40 rifle with a couple of chips in the stock from hard usage. Although there were still a few old Sharps .50 buffalo guns and even a .56 Spencer repeater or two, almost everyone carried the same combination of firearms that Calvin did. The reason was obvious – the shells fit both your handgun and your rifle, and since the cartridge was so popular, they could be had anywhere ammunition was sold.

He followed Pierce back down the steps, the Easterner pausing to lock the door again.

'You will talk to this Lee Trent, won't you?'

'I'll be riding out this morning,' Calvin promised him.

'I won't keep you then,' Darby Pierce said, and the man strode away purposefully toward the table the baron's men had set up for his meal. Calvin watched the man go, removed his hat and scratched at his head. Then, shaking it, he started walking back toward his cabin. He had no good feeling about this, but he was to be paid fifty dollars simply for carrying a message to Lee. He could use that money. Let *Lee* be the one to tell them to go to hell!

Calvin ambled on, passing another wagon and then another. This one had its door open as well and through the opening he caught a glimpse of a lady in black silk. A young lady with eyes of dark blue that shone for an instant like blue sapphires.

She turned her beautiful face toward him and their gazes met for just a moment before a man's hand reached out and slammed the door to the wagon shut. Calvin hesitated and then started on again, a deep frown drawing his features down.

He knew what he had seen, but its significance was lost on him. There was a young woman, watched over by a man, closed up in the wagon away out here in the wilderness.

If that isn't the damnedest thing, he thought. It was none of his business, he knew, and they might resent him even mentioning the girl if they were taking such pains to protect her from prying eyes. Still . . . *it was the damnedest thing.*

TWO

Lee Trent crouched near the edge of the 1,000-foot chalk-colored cliff, looking out across the valley. His horse shifted its feet impatiently, for there was no forage to chew at on this barren bluff. Behind Lee miles of blue spruce, cedar and pine rambled along the rugged terrain of the peaks before they met the bareness of the timberline and were defeated. The breeze was cool, but Trent was not wearing his fringed buckskin jacket. It was tied behind the saddle of the roan.

He wanted to enjoy the last lingering warmth of late summer before the hard weather began. It was not warm where he rested, not at 6,000 feet altitude, but the breathing of the shifting wind was pleasant across his body, only hinting at the chill of evening.

He remained in a crouch, chewing absently at a bit of dried grass. He wore a faded blue shirt, sleeves rolled up to his strong forearms, and black jeans. His shapeless brown hat was tugged low over his eyes. Those eyes were brown and sometimes impenetrable, generally keeping his inner thoughts concealed deeply except when occasional merriment would light them or a dangerous dark mood settled. Then there was no mistaking his meaning.

He looked across the wide valley now. The long grass still flourished, waving in green ripples before the breeze. The little creek that bisected the valley sparkled and shone silver at this distance. Far away the shimmer of the wide and primitive Green River was evident. The valley was half a mile wide and then the land became shadowed by forest once more.

'Someone's coming, Shoshone,' he said to the roan horse. Lee rose to his feet and peered intently into the distance. 'Heading right toward the house. It must be Manassas.'

The roan horse, with a white stocking on its right foreleg and a splash of white on its rump, paid no attention to the human's mutterings. 'It is Manassas,' Trent said. 'I can make out his yellow hound trailing. I wonder what he wants?'

Trent picked up the roan's reins and swung slowly into the saddle. Manassas would wait for him, making coffee if he wished. The trail down to where Lee's house rested was long, narrow and winding. It would take awhile to get there. Lee was in no hurry.

He had paused at the bluff only to look down at his parcel; lonely and wild and free, it was a view he never tired of. His land was almost achingly beautiful. He thought of it as his land, although he did not own it. He had the use of it until he died, and that was all he wanted. He had no descendants and so he did not worry about what happened to it after he was gone. The Cheyenne would reclaim it and he would be only a shadow of memory. He only wanted to live on it in peace. On his own terms, with no man to tell him the laws of civilization.

He started the roan down the trail, winding through the tall timber, listening to the chatter of the gray squirrels bounding from limb to limb, the lonesome caw of a high sailing raven, the squawking of the mountain blue jays. Idly he noticed the tracks of a doe and her fawn where they had crossed a bare patch of ground. Looking high overhead he could see the thin horsetail clouds between the dark pinnacles of the pines.

There was no other place to live, no other way.

Emerging from the pines Lee Trent saw that Manassas had indeed prodded the cookfire to

23

life to boil coffee. In the far country a man was welcome to what he needed. Manassas had made supper for himself many times while he waited for Trent's return from some wandering or other. Frequently, if it had grown dark or the weather was bad, Calvin would also roll up in his blankets in the house to wait for Trent. No one thought anything of it. It was the way guests were treated on the frontier. The latchstring was always out. A man did not leave your house hungry, nor was he put out into the cold. Not so long as he carried the name 'friend'. It was the same with the Indians. Nothing was too good for their friends.

Of course, their enemies did not fare well in this lost land.

Manassas was standing in the open doorway of Trent's cabin, drinking coffee from a blue tin cup. Jack, the yellow hound bellied out to sniff at Lee's boots and to take one cautious smell of Shoshone's hind leg. Shoshone's hoof flicked out, but it was more the gesture of shooing a fly away than with intent to harm the dog.

'Howdy, Lee,' Manassas said, appearing on the porch as Lee swung down, loosely hitched his horse and took his fringed jacket from behind his saddle.

'Hello, Calvin,' the tall man answered. 'Good to see you. Any coffee left?'

'Plenty. I figured you'd be back before long.' Of course, Cal thought, you never knew. The younger man was sometimes gone for days, weeks even, purely on a whim. Calvin thought that Lee Trent felt confined in any building, even his own cabin.

'Any news from down below?' Lee asked as the two men tramped into the cabin.

'Plenty. That's why I'm up this way, Lee. There's things we have to talk about.'

When they were settled at the table, Calvin said, 'There's some hunters at my place. . . .'

'No.'

'You could at least let me tell you, Lee.'

'Tell me what?' Lee asked, sipping at his coffee. 'There's some hunters who want to shoot on my parcel. Otherwise you wouldn't have come out here.' He shook his head 'I won't allow it. Not on my parcel. I never have allowed it; I can't see why I should begin now.'

'Please, Lee. This is different.'

Lee placed his hat aside and rumpled his copper colored hair. 'Go ahead then, Calvin.' He folded his arms on the table and waited for Manassas to say whatever it was that he had come to say. Haltingly Manassas explained about the arrival of the large hunting party, telling Lee the little he knew of the aristocrats and the Baltimore shipping magnate. Lee continued to shake his head negatively.

'I don't believe in hunting for trophies, and you know that,' Trent told his friend.

'Lee,' Manassas replied, leaning farther forward, 'They only want one animal – a trophy sized wapiti.'

'Have you been listening to me?' Lee asked, rising to pour himself another cup of coffee. Calvin's eyes followed the younger man's movement. Out in the field beyond he could see a flock of crows, a dozen or more of them, hopping in circles as they searched for grubs in the long grass. Jack saw them too, and the yellow hound went to the doorway, cocked his big head and watched them, tongue lolling. Lee Trent seated himself again, blowing on the steaming coffee in his cup.

'It's one elk, Lee, that's all. And they're willing to pay you five hundred dollars for a wapiti with a great rack.'

'What are they paying you?' Lee Trent asked. Manassas dropped his eyes in shame.

'Fifty if you let 'em take one wapiti,' Manassas answered.

'They must have money to throw away,' Lee said.

'Lee – they do. But I . . .' Manassas said, 'I don't Lee. Fifty bucks would get me through the winter in fine shape. I could take myself down to Rock Springs and fill my wagon with the needfuls before the snows begin. You could use it too, couldn't you, Lee?' the old man asked hopefully.

'I have all I need,' Trent replied tightly.

'Sure!' Manassas responded. His hands were now clenched tightly, imploring. He was appealing, not trying to convince Lee any longer. 'You have what you need today, Lee. But what about the times which are bound to come? Say Shoshone breaks a leg and you have no horse, say we have a vicious hard winter and you can't find no meat. Say your blankets unravel and there's holes in your boots. Five hundred, Lee,' Manassas said, shaking his head in what was almost a gesture of despair. Lee was thinking about the proposition now, Calvin was sure and he pushed the issue.

'I was thinking,' he said, his gaze meeting Lee Trent's.

'Yes?'

'There's Ulysses, isn't there?'

Ulysses. Yes, Lee thought, there was Ulysses. He was a magnificent bull elk, or had been. He had a harem of fifty does and hundreds of descendants. His antlers were eight feet from point to point. He was a magnificent beast . . . or had been.

'How old do you reckon he is, Lee? I saw him a week or so ago. He can't hardly stagger along with his own herd. His chest hair is turning gray. How old would you say?'

Lee pondered it, looking down at his coffee cup. How old was the great wapiti? Perhaps fifteen or twenty years old. For all of those years he had fought off the jealous younger bull elks, and menacing packs of timber wolves, emerging victorious in his battles, a ruler of his domain.

'Old,' was all Lee said. For no apparent reason the crows took raucously to wing. Lee shifted his eyes to watch them go.

'Lee,' Manassas said intently. 'It'll be a miracle if the old stag can make it through the winter. He ain't strong anymore. The wolves will pull him down, or the herd will leave him behind when they head to the southern valleys. Leave him to starve and freeze in the snow, trying to scramble to his feet and travel with them. Falling, not able to rise. Let the hunters have Ulysses. It'd be a better way for him to go than dying alone out there. At least some good will come of his death this way.'

Lee Trent was silent for a long time. He rose without warning and walked to the door of the cabin to look out at the wide land. Now the skies began to grow heavier with clouds. It would drop close to freezing tonight. Lee, too, had seen Ulysses recently and the magnificent wapiti was on his last legs. He thought of Manassas, needing the money the hunters offered. He took a slow breath and turned back to face his old friend.

'They can have Ulysses. I don't want to see it. I'll miss the old stag,' Lee shrugged, 'but it is time for young blood to take over the herd. Times change and we all age. I guess his time has come at last.'

'It's for the best, Lee,' Manassas said, rising. He put his hat on and started toward the door. He wanted to leave before Lee could change his mind. Inside he felt greedy for the maneuver he was pulling; but it was true that Ulysses could not live much longer. Lee knew it as well.

Lee watched the old man ride away, the yellow dog, its head held low, loping along beside him. Lee went down off the porch to lead Shoshone to his lean-to stable. He rubbed the roan down and filled his rick with new hay. All the time as he worked he thought of Ulysses. He remembered seeing the great wapiti standing on a knoll, his magnificent head with its huge rack, his sleek powerful body backlighted by the dusky orange glow of sunset while his herd – his tribe – grazed in peace across the valley. It was a sight never to be forgotten.

He shook that image from his mind as he walked slowly back toward the cabin. Manassas, after all was right. He didn't want to see the proud creature crippled and harried by wolves, no longer able to fight back. It was only mercy.

Why then did he feel like an executioner?

Calvin Manassas had twinges of guilt himself on his slow ride home. Why, he could not have defined. After all, he had acted only as an inter-mediary and Lee Trent had been free to continue to say 'no'. True, Calvin had brought up Ulysses, but everything he had said was the truth.

There just seemed to be something mercenary about cornering Lee as he had, using Lee for his own gain. Yet he had deceived no one, concealed no fact, omitted nothing.

Except for not telling Lee about the woman in the wagon. Should he have mentioned her? Because Calvin felt that there was something wrong there. Even that uneasy notion he managed to shrug off. It was none of his business. Everyone had secrets of one kind or another. Soon the hunters would be gone as they had come and they would take all their secrets with them. Therefore, Calvin tugged his hat lower in the face of the descending sun and began to whis-tle tunelessly as the yellow dog, tongue lolling, trotted happily beside him.

It was late in the day before Manassas reached his own small ranch. The shadows beneath the oaks and before his horse's legs were long. The days were growing shorter rapidly; it would not be long before purple dusk cloaked the mountains and then after a moment's flare of crimson and orange sunset the light and the shadows would be from the stars and not the sun. Ringed by mountains as they were the abruptness of the change from day to night, heat to chill, could be surprising for the unprepared.

There were only a few men ambling around when Manassas entered his yard. He passed one mounted guard who wore his helmet buckled tightly. Calvin nodded but said nothing. He doubted that the man spoke English anyway. The baron, it seemed, took no chances where his own safety was concerned.

A small array of twinkling lights across the yard puzzled Calvin until he was near enough to see a long table, complete with linen, placed there. The lights were from silver candelabras placed at intervals along the table. Their flickering glow illuminated silver platters and utensils. Calvin stopped, sitting his horse for a long while before, with an amazed shake of his head, he swung down.

Walking his horse toward his cabin he passed the taxidermist, a worried look on his face, standing at the rear of his wagon, the tailgate down. A large inert animal rested on the tailgate and Calvin walked that way.

The animal was a large silver porcupine, over three feet long, bristling with menacing ten-inch long quills along its body and tail. The taxidermist looked at the dead creature this way and that. His hand held a skinning knife but he did not raise it to his work.

'What in hell did they kill a porky for?' Manassas asked in irritation. 'I didn't give anybody the right to shoot on my land!'

'It is ... what?' the confounded taxidermist asked.

'Porcupine,' Calvin said angrily. 'No need to kill it.'

'Like a large hedgehog, is it not?' the man asked helplessly.

'I guess. Never did see a hedgehog myself.'

'What does one do with these?' the exasperated taxidermist asked.

'As little as possible,' Calvin Manassas told him. 'Those quills will break off at a touch and you'll not like it. Ask any dog foolish enough to catch one.'

'Sir,' the foreigner said, holding up a bandaged hand, 'that much I have discovered.'

'Who killed it?'

'The baron. He was bored and thought he might as well kill it when he saw it waddling across your yard.'

Manassas' mouth was tight. It was a waste of a

harmless life. The baron killed because he was bored? Maybe, Calvin reflected, he was making a terrible mistake in having talked to Lee Trent at all. He turned and started away. The taxidermist spoke again.

'Sir, if I may ask. You are familiar with these creatures. How should I . . . what do you think I should do with it?'

'My friend,' Calvin answered. 'Only a fool hunts porcupines. You'd have to be a bigger fool to try skinning it. My advice would be to see that it gets lost before you travel on. I'm inclined to think no one will miss it.'

'Manassas!' a voice called from the dark of the settling dusk and Calvin turned to see Darby Pierce striding toward him, accompanied by a tall, dark man with wavy hair whom Cal had not met before.

'What news?' Darby asked, meeting Calvin as he led his horse to the hitchrail and loosened the cinch.

'Good news for you,' Manassas said with only a trace of bitterness. He studied the second man. He did not know the face, nor did he speak. What kind of civilized world did these people come from anyway – where a man doesn't take your hand, or at least introduce himself?

Cal removed his hat and wiped his brow. 'Let's talk inside, if you don't mind. I need to sit down on something that's not moving.'

Still the other, younger man said nothing, but he followed along into the cabin, standing in the darkness while Manassas fished for a match and lit the kerosene lantern hanging on the wall.

'Want to wait for the baron?' Cal asked, waving out the match.

'Report to me. I can tell the baron all he needs to know,' the young dark man said in a tone that only raised Cal's immediate dislike for him. 'All he wishes to hear is 'yes' or 'no', not to enter into some rambling conversation.'

'Fair enough,' Cal answered, seating himself. He searched his pockets for his pipe and slowly, methodically lit it. Darby Pierce recognized that he was doing it in a manner intended to irritate the foreigner, but the dark-haired man only grew more annoyed, slapping his hand lightly, impatiently against his thigh. Maybe where he came from he was used to having servants anxious to please, and leap to his every command. Maybe he was just plain contrary.

'First off,' Calvin said, lowering himself heavily into his favorite chair, 'I took your message to Lee Trent.'

'We know that!' the foreigner said in exasperation. Darby Pierce interceded.

'He means he wants his fifty dollars,' Darby

said. Cal sat puffing gently on his pipe.

'Gold. American,' Manassas said with a nod.

The European made a sound of disgust and dug into his pockets, tossing a fifty-dollar gold piece onto the table where it rolled toward Cal before hitting a groove in the table. It spun and settled on the tabletop as Calvin watched it without apparent interest.

'What did Trent say?' Darby asked anxiously. *He*, Calvin decided, was extremely interested in pleasing the visitors.

Cal took a minute to prod at his pipe bowl with the burned matchstick. 'He said you can take one bull wapiti,' Manassas said, before the dark man burst a blood vessel with his angry waiting.

'Trophy-sized?' Pierce asked.

'The one he has picked out for you is the largest wapiti any of us has ever seen. Lee says his rack is eight feet from side to side. I'd guess it could even be larger. He carries eighteen points on them. Yes, Lee agrees the baron can hunt this elk if he wishes.'

Pierce looked relieved. The European seemed to relax a little, his dark eyes losing some of their impatient anger.

'I will tell the baron immediately,' the dark man said.

'One minute!' Manassas said, halting the man in stride. 'I did my job. Since you men are going to be rolling on, I'll have to ask for cash on the barrel head.'

'What's he saying?' the foreigner asked Pierce.

'He wants his other fifty dollars,' Pierce said with a weak shrug.

The man muttered another word under his breath. It might have been a muted curse, Cal couldn't tell, but reaching into his pockets again, he stepped forward with another fifty dollar gold piece, slapping it down on the table with the flat of his hand.

'I thank you,' Cal said although he did not reach for the coins.

'If you are satisfied then?'

'Just about,' Cal replied as the man again turned to go. 'You tell the baron one thing for me. This is my land and I can charge for hunting as well as the next man. Tell him that any creature shot here, be it a squirrel or even just a lizard, the price is fifty dollars apiece.'

The nobleman's face blazed with fury, but he said nothing. His eyes raked those of Manassas, but Calvin didn't give him the satisfaction of reacting.

They listened to the man's boot-heels clatter across the sagging porch and be smothered by the night.

'Nice friends you got, Darby,' Cal said.

'You're telling me. I've been on the road with

this bunch since early summer.'

'Why?'

'You have to understand,' Pierce explained. 'These people, the baron especially, are substantial men in the import-export business. My father's shipping company has not been doing well. If we can make connections with the Europeans, we can begin rebuilding. We can trade cotton, furs, timber – you name it – and import tea, ceramics, steel tools our foundries can't replicate. There's a fortune involved. My father is growing old and this may be his last chance to leave us something – me, Mother, my brothers – more than a few rotting hulks sitting at dock. I do have my pride, Manassas. But this is important to my family, very important.'

For the first time Calvin had an insight into Darby Pierce. What he saw now was a desperate, frightened young man, bearing the weight of his family's future on his shoulders.

'I cannot . . .' Pierce said with a slow, deep breath, 'disappoint my father. I cannot alienate these people.'

'I guess I understand,' Calvin said slowly, admiring the young man in a distant way. Though he hated to see Pierce trade his manhood for profit. He rose and walked to the door with Pierce. The silver stars had begun to appear against the purple sky. 'I probably won't see you again after I guide you up to Lee's place, Pierce. Before you go, would you answer one question for me?'

'If I can,' Darby said sincerely.

'Who is the woman in the wagon?'

THREE

'What do you know about her!' Darby Pierce asked. He seemed more embarrassed than upset.

'Nothing,' Calvin Manassas answered, watching the broad Easterner's eyes. 'Except that I saw her once and wondered what a young woman is doing locked up in a wagon.'

Darby appeared confused. The Easterner in his buckskin coat and ironed white shirt looked rumpled and discomfited. He moved his lips but he did not answer. Finally he said quietly, 'Forget you saw her. It has nothing to do with our business.'

In the morning the wagon train with its escort followed Calvin out of the encampment toward the high, broken trail toward Lee Trent's parcel. The wagons proceeded in a ragged column along a winding upward trail. Manassas guided them forward, although once shown the head of the

39

trail the hunting party could have found Trent's cabin on their own.

There were uneasy feelings in Calvin's heart still. Not that he was doing anything criminal or immoral, but that he had made a wrong decision based on his own needs. He was not, that is to say, particularly proud of bringing this collection of men of dubious character into Lee Trent's wilderness sanctorum.

The pines massed large and dark, rubbing against each other's boughs as the caravan trailed higher. The scent of the evergreens was almost overpowering. The sky became only a strip of brilliant blue above the trail. The men who rode with Manassas were silent for the most part. The baron with his sweeping mustache, flanked by his two helmeted guards, the insolent dark man and Darby Pierce in buckskins and a crimson shirt appearing subdued himself. Behind them trailed the wagons, clanking, squeaking, flanked by various outriders – taxidermist, dogsbodies and kitchen help on stumpy, heavy-coated horses, and behind them a half-dozen men whose function was not clear but whom Manassas took to be other fighting men.

These last were a rough assortment without uniforms, probably collected here and there across the frontier to further insure the baron's safety in the wilds. Judging only by their dress they seemed to be Americans, but the hunters had been long in the West and maybe they had simply adapted to local custom.

At last the party broke from the woods and before them was a wide, long-grass valley and a silver rill with Lee Trent's three-room log cabin in the distance, set back against the face of a rising bluff.

'From what this man had said, I expected a great manor,' the baron said to the younger, dark man. Manassas glanced at them, his expression wooden.

'This land, though,' the baron said with a sweeping gesture. 'All his? Even to the mountains.'

'That's right,' Calvin answered.

'Then he must be a very good friend of the Cheyenne indeed.'

'Yes, sir,' Calvin said using the term of address not out of respect or obeisance, but from habit. His father had taught Calvin that it costs nothing to call a man 'sir.' 'He is a brother and a son to Great Elk, the chief of the Green River Cheyenne.'

'So—' Baron Stromberg said thoughtfully, tugging at his huge mustache. 'How did this come about?'

'That's not for me to say, sir. I don't know the half of it. Lee,' he shrugged, 'he don't like to talk about it a lot.'

'I see.'

'Pierce,' Cal said to the American. 'I might not have done as good a job as I should of explaining to Trent how many people there were in this hunting party. At any rate, I think maybe just you and the baron and ... whoever this fellow is, should ride up to the house with me. You can look around and see there's plenty of grass for the animals, plenty of water for your needs. Your people ought to hold back here in the meadows while we settle the finer points with Trent.'

'I understand,' Darby Pierce said. 'Baron?'

'Yes, yes, I understand,' Stromberg said. The man was in a subdued state of excitement, and it gave Calvin pause to consider. Why was this world-wide hunter so wrought up over a chance to bag one more animal to display in the halls of his baronial mansion? There was something. . . .

'Do we go now?' the dark-haired man wanted to know. His irritation continued to chafe Calvin's sensibilities. No matter – he would soon be shucked of all of them and then he could make his way downriver to Rock Springs for his winter stores. When he came back, they would be gone, winter would be arriving and things would be back to normal once more.

'We'd better,' Manassas said, squinting toward the cabin. 'I can see Lee standing on his porch now, probably wondering what's keeping us.'

In a file the four men started toward Lee Trent's home. Jack broke away from them and ran toward Trent, barking twice to announce himself. When they swung down from their horses, Lee Trent was crouched, petting the eager dog's head. Lee looked them over in silence, then rose.

'You may as well come inside, gentlemen,' the frontiersman said.

Manassas said, 'I'll just wait out here, Lee. I've got nothing to do with the rest of your business.'

Darby Pierce considered for a moment. 'Neither do I. I'll wait out here with Manassas.'

The baron impatiently strode into the house, paying little attention to the cabin or its occupant. These were only stepping stones to his objective. The young dark-haired man followed, managing to swagger in riding boots. Manassas sat down on the porch, wiped his salt and pepper hair back and replaced his hat. Darby seated himself beside Calvin and the two studied the wide valley and the far snowcapped mountains in companionable silence.

'Who is that whelp, anyway?' Manassas asked, nodding toward the closed door of the cabin.

'The duke?'

'If that's what he is,' Calvin shrugged.

'His name is Duke Severin Caulfield von Hefflen.'

'Is that what you call him?' Manassas asked with a tight smile. Darby smiled in return.

'I don't call him anything – you see how he is.'

'How'd he come to be here? Important man, is he?'

'In his own mind. His family once held a duchy in Bavaria. It's long since gone as a legal state, but he's entitled to call himself "duke".'

Calvin shrugged and slowly filled his pipe. He knew nothing about European duchies and only a little about the geography in those foreign lands. Darby still hadn't answered his question.

'So – what brings him out here on the expedition?'

'You haven't figured it? Well, as you saw there is a young woman, a very beautiful young lady travelling with the hunting party. Her name is Lucinda – she's the baron's daughter.'

'Oh?' Manassas said, things beginning to clarify themselves in his mind. He puffed lazily at his pipe and scratched the dog's ears. 'And Duke – whatcha may call him—'

'Is engaged to Lucinda. He's trying desperately to recover his station in life, you see, Calvin. We've passed into a time different from those of his ancestors. Now it's money and not land that counts among the aristocracy. He will never recover his duchy, and he knows it, but—'

'By marrying the baron's daughter, he might well gain a lot of money.'

Darby nodded. Manassas was unlettered, but he had a quick grasp of matters. Broodingly the young American studied the distant camp where several cook fires had been started. After all, he had to admit, wasn't he doing the same thing as the duke? Hoping to pry gold from the baron's fingers. He considered that unhappily for a moment and then decided that his was a more noble motive. Besides, he and his father's shipping line were offering a service for their share of the baron's vast wealth, a service that should be mutually advantageous.

Calvin interrupted his thoughts. 'So . . . the woman? Why is she a prisoner in the camp, Darby? Are they afraid that she might try to run away? Afraid that harm might come to her out in the wilderness? Try to leave the duke before they can be married?'

'No,' the man from Baltimore answered without glancing at Manassas. 'I thought you might have guessed, that you somehow knew . . . Lucinda Stromberg is quite mad.'

Inside the cabin Lee Trent watched the eyes of the two men as they reached an understanding. Ulysses could be taken; Lee would guide them to

45

the herd himself. If the baron was actually willing to pay $500 for the trophy, then under the circumstances he and Calvin had discussed, it was – sadly – time to let the old stag travel on to another life. That is where the Cheyenne believed the elk went. It was customary to apologize to the animals before they were hunted down, to assure them that there was a bright trail in the sky for them to follow to a better land.

Lee Trent, who had been much among the Indians, was not convinced of that, but he hoped that there was a wisdom among the Cheyenne he had not yet grasped fully.

'When can we proceed?' was the duke's stiff question. Lee's eyes revealed nothing, but he found himself not liking the young nobleman already. That had been Calvin's first impression, but Lee didn't let other people's opinions color his own. Hearing that someone is no good leads to carrying that prejudice into a meeting. But now he saw what Manassas had meant.

Lee spoke to the baron who had not shifted position since entering the cabin except to occasionally toy with his huge mustache. 'We can scout the herd in the morning. There shouldn't be more than a few of us. We don't want to spook the elk. If you have field-glasses you'll be able to study Ulysses at range and assure yourself that he is indeed trophy size.'

'I don't doubt your word,' the baron insisted. 'When may I have my shot at him?'

Lee hesitated and then shrugged, 'Bring your chosen weapon tomorrow. It may be the elk will shy; it may be Ulysses will offer us a clean shot.'

Even as he spoke Lee Trent felt traitorous toward the big wapiti. He sighed inwardly. Such thoughts did nothing to help. The bargain had been made, logically and monetarily. He would deliver up the great creature. The stack of fifty-dollar gold pieces on the table gleamed dully in the lantern light, but Lee Trent seemed not to notice them. He rose and indicated silently that he was finished with the discussion and the two Europeans went out.

Troubled by the turn of events which he himself had allowed to eventuate, Lee Trent rose after a few minutes and went out himself, leaving the stack of coins where they rested. Really, they meant little to him. Although as Manassas had pointed out, gold does have its uses, especially if hard times befell him.

Calvin was still seated on the porch, his pipe bowl showing a small red coal, a lazy stream of smoke rising into the late afternoon sky.

'Well, Lee,' the old man said, patting a place on the porch beside him, 'what do you think?'

Lee sat with his hands clasped, looking toward the camp the hunters had set up on his meadow.

'You know what I think, Calvin.'

'I guess I do,' Manassas said, glancing at the younger man. 'It seemed like the thing to do at the time. There's so many things that seem that way,' he added with a wry smile. 'Nope – I don't know. You would likely have shot old Ulysses yourself if you saw him having trouble this winter.'

'Likely,' Lee agreed. 'It doesn't make a man feel any better.'

'No,' Manassas agreed. 'These people,' he said, waving his pipe toward the encampment. 'What do they even know about life out here? You know, Lee, I doubt a one of them could survive a winter in Wyoming. Without their fancy weapons and supplies. I think, Lee, that we're coming to a time when people won't even know how to clothe themselves or feed themselves, build a shelter, if someone else doesn't provide the labor.' It was a deep thought for Manassas, and he shook his head at the implacable progression of time.

The sun had tilted over toward the western hills; the Rocky Mountains, their high reaches lost in eternal ice, grew dark and withdrew into the solemnity of coming night. Lee Tent rose from the porch and dusted off his britches.

'Pardon me, Calvin, if you will,' he said, 'I feel the need to be by myself for a while.'

Calvin nodded, and watched as the strong young man walked slowly away, entering the fringes of the forest where all was shadow and the only sounds the sad song of the night birds.

Lee Trent walked on, following a path he had known by heart for years. It was there that he had first found Four Dove, the lovely Cheyenne girl only half his age who had been wounded by encroaching Shoshone Indians.

The baron had asked earlier how a friend of the Cheyenne could name his horse 'Shoshone.' And, studying the nobleman with his expressionless brown eyes, Lee had told him a part of the story. Not all of it; he had told no man all of it.

'The horse's name is in memory of the skirmish. Great Elk gave him to me and so it was named for the six Shoshones who lay dead in this forest.'

The baron had said nothing. Duke von Hefflen's face carried the mocking expression of a man whose exploits had been exaggerated, so believed no one else's. It had not mattered to Lee Trent what they thought. A question had been asked and answered; let them believe what they liked. Lee did not walk through his life to impress others.

Now and then he thought of Four Dove. Of the long trek when he had carried her with her legs torn and her body bruised, through the snow the six miles to the Cheyenne camp. That was when he had won his 'parcel' from Great Elk although he had never asked for a reward.

How old would the girl be by now? My God! She would be a young woman, nineteen or twenty, probably married to a strong young buck with three or four chubby little children crawling around her lodge . . . or so he hoped. So he liked to envision her life.

He had not been back to the Cheyenne camp for five years. Shoshone – the horse must be nearly nine years old now! Lee shook his head. The years were sliding away. Each day seemed so long at times, but the years flowed as rapidly as the Green River careening through the gorge.

Lee's thoughts, focused on the past were jolted suddenly into the urgency of the present as a young woman in black silk burst from the forest depths and threw herself into his arms.

'Help me,' she said. 'Oh, please help me escape from them!'

The night was settling softly, the sky a rich purple. Lee was not a hundred yards from where he had found Four Dove and rescued her from an attacking party of Shoshones. There was a moment when the sudden appearance of the dark-haired, slight woman caused him to wonder if he had re-entered a dream. But she drew her face away from his shoulder and he saw her blue eyes, the pale flesh and the moment of *déjà vu* vanished.

'Who. . . ?' He put her at arm's length and examined her. Who indeed, was this woman?

'They wouldn't have told you,' the woman said shaking her head violently. 'I am Lucinda. Did you hear me! I have escaped and you must help me find freedom.'

'Lady—'

'Please,' Lucinda begged, her eyes meeting his, falling away and returning. 'I am a prisoner. I know that this is your estate – I have heard them talking – I know you are the lord of the manor. I pray, give me protection.'

Lee stood stunned by this outpouring of myth and fabrication. Unprepared, he tried to explain. 'I'm lord of nothing, miss. I have no estate. I am a man of the wild country, that is all.'

'All the better!' the girl with the deep blue eyes said excitedly. 'Then you know all the better how to protect me from . . . them,' she said, gesturing toward the distant camp.

'No. I don't know how to do that, nor why I should.'

'Sir!'

'If you'll calm down a little so that we can talk, maybe I can help you in some way,' Lee tried to explain, 'but I can't barge into affairs that I know nothing about. Please,' he said to the girl with the violently rising and falling breath, 'tell me something I can understand, and we'll see if we can't

51

find some solution to matters.'

'Is there a place. . . ?' Lucinda asked, looking around.

'I have a small cabin not far from here. I lived in it before I built the big house,' Lee said, smiling at the term. The 'big house' had three rooms and a wooden roof. The cabin had one room and a pine bough ceiling and had been abandoned after the first needful winter he had occupied the Cheyenne land. 'Come along,' he said to the woman who shivered beneath her dress and clung tightly to him.

You see, he would have told Manassas, had he been there, this is what a man gets for allowing strangers on his parcel.

They wove their way through the dense pines and blue spruce toward the disused cabin on the rocky ledge. Interlaced as they were, someone might have taken them for lovers; the truth was that Lee could not get Lucinda to release her grip on him, and she was staggering as she walked beside him in her town shoes, tripping over roots and loose rocks so that he felt a need to support her. Lee liked none of it, although he had to admit if there were anyone there to admit it to, that the warmth of her body beneath her black silk dress was pleasing against him.

She tripped again and then began to stagger.

She had to pause and lean her back against a pine tree, hands behind her. Overhead the sky was growing rapidly dark and the stars began to blink on one by one. Through the deep forest Lee could no longer even see the camp-fires.

'I need to know—' he began, and the girl buried her face in her hands and began weeping so that her shoulders shook.

'I can't tell you all,' she said tearfully. 'They have me prisoner. It is because I won't marry Severin – Duke von Hefflen. There is an important financial transaction between him and my father.' She lowered her head in shame, 'And I . . . I am a part of the price.'

'We'd better get you inside,' Lee said. He was shivering with the cold himself, having come out wearing only a shirt. The night would grow no warmer; he guessed the thermometer, had they one, would stand near thirty degrees. The young woman in her silk dress was certainly cold.

He urged her toward the tiny cabin, assisting her by supporting an arm. Then, in the near darkness as she collapsed Lee scooped her up and carried her in his arms, placing her on the rickety bed which had been his own once and now showed signs of age. A leather strap had broken and one leg was angled like that of a spavined horse. No matter – she would be better off here than out in the forest. He wasn't sure he could have made his way back to camp carrying her; and he did not know what punishment might await her there.

The old grizzly bearskin still rested in the chest near the door. It had a stale scent to it, but it would keep her very warm. Lee himself stood looking down at her placid, beautiful features and shook his head with uncertainty. He had needed no further complications with these people and their mysterious ways. Yet now he had brought her here; he would let her rest for the night and maybe tomorrow her story would be clearer and he could decide on a proper course of action.

He, of course, had not been made privy to the conversation between Manassas and Darby Pierce. No one had told him that the girl was considered to be a madwoman.

Lee took an Indian blanket which hung on the wall and wrapped it around him as he sat in the cabin's only chair, his boots propped up on the low table. It was cold and uncomfortable, but then he had passed many nights in the mountains with fewer comforts.

Outside an owl screeched and a distant coyote barked excitedly. The night passed in cold progression and Lee Trent fell gradually into a restless sleep.

*

He had seen the girl running as swiftly as a fawn in flight. As slender and as graceful, her huge dark eyes filled with terror, her mouth set determinedly. She wove through the tall pines, flitting from shadow to shadow. She passed near enough for him to hail her, but she did not pause in her headlong rush. She was Cheyenne – that was clear from her dress – and very young, on the verge of budding into womanhood, but still a frightened child. He thought that she might have encountered a mountain lion or an irritable grizzly; then not fifty feet behind her he saw the attackers.

The Shoshones were afoot and Lee reined in the stocky gray horse he rode in those years, lifting his Henry repeater as a warning.

In the passion of their frenzied pursuit, the Shoshones did not even slow at the unexpected appearance of the tall white man. The man second from the lead dropped to one knee and fired his rifle wildly at Lee. It was a near miss and Lee Trent had answered with a shot from his Henry repeater which slammed the Indian back to land roughly against the ground, his heart stopped. Then a howl went up from the attacking Shoshones and as one they wheeled toward Lee.

An arrow caught the thick-shouldered gray horse in the chest and it leaped forward, shook its head crazily and collapsed. Lee just managed to kick free of the stirrups before the animal rolled, kicked at the air and died. Lee leapt forward to use the horse's body as a breastwork. From behind the heated body of the horse he fired into the chest of an onrushing Shoshone and the man folded up in mid-stride to fall to the earth.

To his left Lee heard another attacker howl and saw that this warrior was still pursuing the fleeing woman fifty yards down the slope of the wooded hillside. From a seated position Lee carefully trained his sights on the man, led him with the front bead of the Henry and fired. The Shoshone brave halted in his tracks, looked in confusion to the right and left and then collapsed.

Lee turned his eyes back toward his attackers in time to see another warrior leap the horse like a hurdling athlete, lance held high, ready to strike. Lee could see the man's painted face, his determined eyes clearly as he pulled the trigger of his repeater and shot the man in mid-vault. The Shoshone fell, so near that his feathered lance brushed Lee Trent's arm as he somersaulted to his death.

The Indian had pinned Lee's legs to the ground and he slithered free as yet another young buck burst from the pine forest, his scream angry and determined. Lee, still on his back, levered another round into the chamber of the Henry and fired wildly. He heard rather than saw the Shoshone fall and he lay back, breathing deeply.

Wriggling from under the weight of the dead Indian he turned over and began crawling away from the bloody scene.

The Shoshone's moccasin came down on the barrel of his rifle and Lee looked up to see the grim, violent face of yet another warrior. Lee rolled to one side and tried to scramble to his feet, but the Indian, wielding a steel tomahawk rushed upon him and the two men went down in a cloud of dust among the strewn pine needles.

Lee clamped his left hand around the Shoshone's wrist before he could drive his axe down into his skull. Flailing wildly with his own left hand, the Indian tried to batter Lee's head into the ground. Lee was the larger man and he managed to roll on top of the raider, pinning his shoulders with his knees.

'Give it up. There has been enough death,' Lee said using the smattering of the Shoshone tongue he knew, but the man would not quit.

'It is done!' Lee said in English, but it had no effect on the violently writhing young Shoshone.

The near report of a rifle shocked Lee's eardrums. Smoke wreathed their small war site. The Indian's mouth gaped and blood flowed from it. The man tried to frame a few words, could not, and lay back dead.

Lee looked up to see the girl, no more than thirteen or fourteen, holding his own rifle, a wisp of smoke curling from its muzzle still. She was panting with the rapidity of a small hunted animal. Her face was streaked with scratches from her rush through the forest. Her legs were both bloody; her white elkskin shirt had been torn open. Her eyes were as dark as obsidian, her hair, tangled with briers was as black as midnight in winter. She collapsed to the ground and Lee carried her home to the tiny cabin in the woods. She had said, 'My name is Four Dove and you are my man,' and then passed out in his arms as he placed her on the small bed he had made and covered her with the warm hide of a rogue grizzly bear he had killed only the week before.

Lee awoke.

There was a woman in his bed. Who? He stretched and waited for the recollection to come back, for dream and reality to sort themselves out.

Slowly, through the dense fog of heavy sleep, he realized that he had had the long dream again. The dream of Four Dove.

Now he rose, stiff with the cold. He stood over the foreign woman, watching the twitch of long eyelashes, the tight gripping of her hands as she slept. Then he walked to the doorway and stepped outside for a long while, watching the dream of a thousand stars.

FOUR

Lee Trent emerged from the cabin as morning colored the long skies. He had covered the sleeping woman's bare shoulder with the bearskin and looked down at her for a long moment before he shrugged and went out, closing the door behind him.

He made his way back toward his home over bundles of pine needles glossed with ice. Beyond the trees, ground fog rose from the grassy expanse. The valley was strewn with millions of dewy prisms. There was smoke rising from early fires in the hunters' camp and now and then the sound of utensils banging against pots.

Manassas, looking drawn and haggard met him before he could reach the cabin.

'Where have you been, Lee? You had me worried.'

'I've just been dreaming,' Lee told him.

'Huh?' the old man was deeply perplexed.

'Never mind,' Lee said with a dismissive gesture. 'It doesn't matter.'

'The baron is ready to go, Lee. He's been looking for you everywhere.'

'Well,' Lee shrugged, 'here I am.'

Manassas followed the longer-legged man quickly as he strode down the grassy slope. 'The baron and them were up half the night,' Calvin told Lee Trent. 'Something has happened, though they wouldn't let on what it was.'

Lee only nodded as Calvin waited for an informative answer. None was forthcoming. Finally, not far from his front door, Lee asked, 'Calvin, does everything travel in cycles? Like the planets or the moon constantly revolving, I mean. Does everything happen twice?'

Manassas had no answer, did not understand what sort of answer he was supposed to make. 'Never mind,' Lee said, resting his hand on the old mountain man's shoulder. 'It was just a notion.'

'You must have had a hell of a dream,' Manassas said.

Shoshone whickered from his stable. The big roan either had heard them or simply realized that it was time for breakfast. Beyond the house someone was waving furiously toward them. Lee ignored the man as he went to fork some hay for

Shoshone. Manassas followed, his mind still mulling Lee's strange questions.

Manassas leaned against the rails of the small corral, watching Lee toss hay into the rick in Shoshone's lean-to barn. When Lee was finished, leaning the fork against the wall of the shelter, he turned back toward Manassas, his eyes searching the sky, finding them calm, unthreatening.

'The baron is in a hurry, Lee,' Calvin said.

Lee nodded. 'He strikes me as the kind of man who's always in a hurry, getting nowhere.'

'You did promise him,' Manassas reminded him.

Lee smiled slightly. 'I know what I'm doing, Cal. I don't like it, but I know what I'm doing.'

Abashed, Calvin said, 'Sorry, Lee. I know that. I've got nothing more to do with this anyway, and I know you can handle these foreigners.'

'I'm hoping so,' Lee said. He rolled down his sleeves and came out the gate, repositioning the wire loop that held the gate posts. Shoshone swiveled one ear toward him and glanced at him briefly. 'Don't worry,' Lee said quietly to the horse, 'you'll get some exercise today. I won't leave you behind.' He walked up beside Manassas and placed one boot on the lowest rail of the corral. 'Cal,' he said, 'I need some help.'

'Do you?' the older man said. 'I thought something was on your mind.'

'When do you plan on heading out for Rock Springs?'

'I dunno, Lee. Today, tomorrow . . .'

'Why don't you make it today? Hitch your team and bring your wagon up here after I've gone with the baron.'

'Well,' Calvin said thoughtfully, 'I don't see any reason why not – the thing is, why? If you don't mind me asking.'

'I want you to take someone with you,' Lee said, glancing back toward the hunters' camp.

'You mean – say, Lee, have you got that Lucinda girl they're looking all over hell for?'

'I've got her. She's stashed away up at the old place. She told me they've been keeping her prisoner.'

'Uh-huh,' Calvin slowly took his pipe from the pocket of his greasy leather coat and lit it. 'Did she also tell you that they think she's insane, Lee? That's the way I got the story, that she's plain mad.'

'Who told you that?'

'Darby Pierce.'

'You trust that man?' Lee wanted to know. Calvin shrugged his thin shoulders.

'I've kinda started to warm up to him now that I know him a little. I don't know if it's the truth – it could be that that's just what they told him.'

An owl, flying late in the morning, swooped low

overhead on wide wings, its talons clenching a red weasel and disappeared into the dark forest. Only the very tips of the tallest pines were lit by the sun rising beyond the Rocky Mountain peaks. Shoshone tossed his head and went to his water bucket.

'Are you saying you want no part of her?' Lee asked flatly.

'Not particularly,' Calvin answered honestly, 'but if you think it's the right thing to do, why, I'll take her south with me.'

Lee replied with some frustration, 'I think if she wants to go, then she should be allowed to. She's got family and friends where she comes from. Riding around in a locked wagon out here . . . it's just plain cruel, Cal.'

'Tell me what you want, Lee. I'll do it.'

'First – after we've pulled out, find her and ask if she wants to go home. If she does, stow her in your wagon and take her to Rock Springs. She can ferry down the Green River and make her way to Denver and then east from there. There's five hundred dollars on the table in my cabin. That's plenty for her to get to the East Coast and book passage to wherever she wants to go.'

'The money. . . ?'

'I didn't have it before they got here and I got along, didn't I?' Lee spread his hands. Actually the money meant almost nothing to him. He just wanted the girl to be safe and be able to return home if that was what she wanted. 'Just make sure she hasn't changed her mind – a woman can be notional – and if not, help her get to Rock Springs.'

Calvin was studying Shoshone as if he had never seen a horse before. His eyes were narrowed, his teeth clenched on his old briar pipe. 'If that's what you want, Lee. If that's what she wants.' He shrugged again. 'She seems to be over twenty-one. Crazy or not, she should have the right to make a choice.'

'Trent!'

Lee turned at the sound of Duke von Hefflen's throaty hail. The duke was wearing loose twill trousers and a white poplin shirt this morning. A gray Stetson shadowed his eyes. There was another man with him, a lanky man of thirty or so wearing faded blue jeans and a red shirt. He had a thin mustache and pale green eyes. Lee frowned. He thought he had seen the man the day before. He was one of a type, he thought.

Lee took him for a Texas cowhand who had gotten tired of pushing longhorn steers for a dollar a day, weary of the stink and danger of it and, having no other real skills and approaching middle age, had become one of the wolves who roamed the West looking to make a living with their guns alone. Lee turned and straightened to greet the duke.

'I don't suppose you've seen her?' the duke asked and Lee drew his eyebrows together questioningly.

'Who?'

'Lucinda – never mind, you wouldn't know her name. There was a young woman with our train. Now she's gone.'

'You oughta watch them a little closer,' Lee said. There was no real humor in his voice and his comments were accepted without any.

'Never mind, Trent. It doesn't concern you. I'll find her. Where can she go – out here?' He waved an arm taking in the vastness of the wild country. 'The baron is getting impatient, however; he says we should have been on the trail hours ago.'

'How would he know that?' Lee Trent asked. 'I believe this part of the hunt has been left up to me. I know where the wapiti are bedded and I know where they graze. The baron has nothing to get impatient over. I'll be down to see him soon.' All this time Lee had been studying the man he took for a Texan, from the way he slouched to one side as he stood, to the way he wore his gun just a few inches too low, from the cocky expression on his sunburned face. Now the man spoke.

'You know me?' he demanded.

'I don't think so,' Lee answered.

'The name's John Saturday,' the Texan said

with just a hint of boastfulness.

'Fine-sounding name,' Lee said, and he nodded before re-entering the corral to smooth Shoshone's blanket on the roan's back before saddling up. Saturday stood staring at Lee, his thumbs hooked behind his cartridge-laden gunbelt. Once Lee glanced at Manassas but Calvin only shrugged. Perhaps the gunhand was a big shot where he came from, or thought of himself as one, but Texas was far, far away from the Wapiti Range.

With Shoshone saddled, Lee returned to the cabin to gulp down a cup of the dark coffee Manassas had boiled that morning. Calvin, himself, was already gone, heading toward his cabin to hitch his wagon and deliver Lucinda to Rock Springs where, free of her, Cal would do his winter stores shopping and return home.

Lee stood in the doorway, sipping from his tin cup as the hunters' wagons were hitched and the body of men moved toward his yard. Frowning, Lee placed the cup away and waited, hands on hips as they approached through the chill morning. Why were they bringing the wagons? He had advised the baron that no more than three or four men would be useful on the hunt, but now they had three wagons rolling and no less than ten men.

No matter, Lee thought, and in a growly mood

he closed his front door, reached his roan and swung aboard Shoshone. Whatever the baron had in mind was fine. Anything! Just so they got their trophy and departed, leaving him to the peace of his mountain parcel.

Darby Pierce, still wearing a buckskin jacket over a white shirt and black jeans, separated himself from the group and rode to meet Lee Trent, his broad face appearing apologetic.

'Sorry,' Darby said, reining in beside Lee. 'I tried reminding the baron what you had said, but you know how he is. I might as well have been talking to a brick wall.'

'It's all right,' Lee replied to the man from Baltimore. 'I guess he's just plain too used to having his own way in everything.'

'I heard him tell the duke that he wanted men with him because there were likely to be Indians around.'

'The only Indians around are Cheyenne – and even they don't violate my boundaries,' Lee answered. He started the splash-flanked roan forward and Darby stayed beside him. The morning remained cool as would the day. The lingering autumn was rapidly fading. 'Who is this John Saturday?' Lee asked. 'And what of these Texans riding with him?'

'Johnny Saturday?' Darby responded with surprise. 'Why we were told he was a sharp eyed

scout and a renowned Indian fighter. The others
. . . well, they're his hand-picked crew.'

Lee said nothing. He had never heard of John
Saturday. Despite the vast distances in the West,
really famous men like Hickok, Kit Carson, John
Wesley Hardin, all had reputations that were
carried in tales told around the camp-fire. John
Saturday's was not one of these. He must have
spun a believable story to the baron, however, for
here he was.

The two men rode in silence for more than a
mile as Lee found one nearly hidden trail after
another through the secret depths of the pines.
The wagons would have trouble following their
path, and Darby wondered if Lee was doing it on
purpose, but he did not ask the mountain man to
share his thoughts.

'They couldn't find Lucinda,' Darby said eventually as the yellow sun burst above the ice-capped
mountains and lit the long valleys below.

'No?' Trent said with little apparent interest. 'Is
she anything to you, Pierce?'

Pierce laughed. 'No, sir. I have a woman back
home who is kind and gentle to all people,
animals – she is waiting to marry me once I've
gotten the baron finished with his Western safari
and has signed the contracts with my father's
shipping line.'

Trent nodded. He was beginning to see what

Manassas meant. He, too, was warming to the young Easterner who seemed to be caught up in a manipulative web not of his devising.

'Is she crazy?' Lee asked from out of the blue and Darby's eyes widened, flickering to Lee's.

'Lucinda, you mean?'

'Yes. I have heard tales that she is mad.'

Darby thought that over carefully. 'I don't think so,' he answered at length. 'I mean, I don't know her at all. It would be strange if she wasn't terribly distressed – being hauled over vast distances in a foreign land that must seem nearly uninhabitable to her. Locked in a wagon for thousands of miles.' He carefully added, 'She may be. By now – after all she's endured. You know, of course, that she is betrothed to the duke?'

'I know it,' Lee said tightly. 'With parents like that . . . it makes you wonder what kind of a child they might produce.'

Lee reined in and pointed ahead. 'You see that piney ridge? Beyond it is where the elk bed down. There's a small grassy valley over the rise. Tell the baron that we cannot take the wagons any farther – the wapiti will be bound to hear the axles creaking. Also, tell him that those guards of his, the ones with the shiny helmets, will have to remain behind or remove them. Sunlight on the helmets will alert the elks.'

'I understand,' Darby responded. 'Tell him

yourself – here he comes.'

Baron Stromberg and the duke were riding toward them at a canter, the baron on his white stallion, the duke astride that glossy black gelding. Lee awaited them with shallow patience. He had to remind himself constantly that they were nearly at the beginning of the hunt and the end of any relationship with these two men. He repeated what he had told Darby Pierce and the baron nodded, stroking his fantastic white mustache.

'You advise then that we proceed on foot?'

'Yes, sir. Give me ten minutes to crest the rise and try locating Ulysses, then we can proceed. You, I assume, are the shooter.'

'Of course,' the baron said with a shadow of indignation.

Lee nodded his head. 'Then check and load your chosen weapon. I'll be back as soon as I can.' Swinging down from Shoshone's back, Lee entered the woods, clambered up the slope and paused among the pines, going to his belly to look out across the valley.

There stood the wapiti stag – proud and imperial, the master of all within his domain. Ulysses had been drinking from the narrow silver rill, but now at some small sound, he lifted his muzzle and water dripped in pearl-like beads from his mouth. His rack was exquisite. Lee's outstretched arms could not have matched their breadth. Ulysses had long surveyed the land, long protected his herd, long sired sleek, strong young. Now it was his time to pass from the earth, and without shame Lee felt his eyes cloud. He slithered back down the ridge.

'He's there,' he told the baron. 'It's a two-hundred yard shot from here. If you want to wait and see if they drift nearer . . .'

'Are you questioning the baron's shooting ability?' the always abrasive Duke von Hefflen demanded.

'I am questioning nothing,' Lee said, keeping the lid on any sharp retort he may have wished to make. 'It's just that patience is sometimes required for a sure kill.'

'I do not miss,' the baron said coldly, and that was that.

The duke carried the .45-.90 Belgian rifle that Manassas had seen earlier in the armory wagon. The baron himself was handed a bench rifle such as Lee had never seen. Bench rifles, as they are called, are named that because they are too heavy for a man to shoulder and fire easily and with accuracy. A few of these had been used by snipers during the War Between the States. They weighed between fourteen and forty pounds and were meant to be fired from a sniper's 'bench', a tree trunk, a stump. A boulder. This one, although

Lee did not recognize it, was a British-made .45 Whitworth which was said in brochures to have a 'killing accuracy' of 1,500 yards. It was fitted with a barrel-length 4X-power scope. The weapon was not a sporting rifle, Lee noted grimly, but a killing device. Ulysses was not being hunted. The great wapiti was being executed.

'You all right, Trent?' Darby Pierce asked.

'Sure. I made the bargain, didn't I?' he answered. And he was suddenly pleased that he would earn no tainted gold from this bloody expedition, that he had given the money to Manassas for the woman. Lucinda, whatever she was, could not be as mad as these hunters.

'Follow me. Silently,' Lee cautioned. He was now aware that the Texans and a few of the baron's entourage were surrounding them, prepared to proceed with the hunting party.

'We don't need all these people with us,' Lee said to the baron. The nobleman ignored him completely, instead summoning a man who trotted forward with a brace which Lee assumed was a shooting stand for the baron's huge octagonal-barreled rifle.

Through clenched teeth, Lee said, 'Let's go, gentlemen,' and began to work his way upslope again, the pine and cedar trees feeling close and the shadows cold. There was no birdsong to be heard in all of the long forest.

Achieving the ridge, Lee gestured the others to silence and they moved stealthily to a small overhang Lee had chosen for the hunter's bench. The gun bearers moved forward, two intent Scotsmen, and they drove the upright rest with its U-shaped wooden brace into the pine-needle-littered ground with padded mallets.

The wapiti herd had not been alerted and they continued to graze in pastoral calm. The baron had focused his field-glasses on Ulysses and Lee saw a twitch beneath his vast white mustache which might have been a smile. The baron handed the binoculars to Duke von Hefflen and then, keeping his eyes fixed on the elk herd, he moved to the rest where his Manchester-tooled Whitworth .45 awaited him. One of the expressionless Scots had positioned the baron's shooting camp chair and now the portly man seated himself, watching the herd for long moments through the telescopic sight attached to his rifle. His mouth hung open a little at the urge toward blood. Lee Trent turned away, unwilling to watch and went a little way into the deep shadows of the forest verge, his eyes lifted to the far blue mountains.

The crack of the rifle caused him to flinch as its brutal echo rolled across the valley.

It was over then!

But it wasn't – on the heels of the baron's shot

came another dozen and then tens of dozens of rounds behind fired. Lee ran toward the site to find all of the baron's entourage firing a savage volley of gunfire at the herd. Does and young fawns fell to the earth, ran in confused circles of futile escape or pawed madly on broken limbs trying to escape the slaughter. Lee Trent saw John Saturday, grinning widely, emptying his six-shooter into the panicked herd.

An atavistic howl rose in Lee's throat. He did not know if he ever voiced the sound. No one could have heard it above the roar of the guns anyway. It seemed to him that the cry clogged his throat like a burning ember and spread fury through his chest. Betrayed, he leaped forward wildly, trying to get his hands on the duke's throat as the laughing nobleman reloaded his rifle calmly. Hurling himself that way through the sheet of gunpowder that fanned across the hillside, Lee felt a blow like a sledge hammer striking against the base of his skull. He twisted as he fell, believing that he saw John Saturday, still grinning like the devil, standing over him with his pistol. He could not be sure it was Saturday who had clubbed him down; he could be sure of nothing in the confusion.

Lee saw a shadowy man standing over him and he leg-whipped him, taking the man's legs out from under him before he crawled frantically away toward the forest. He got to his feet as men pursued him. He reached for his holster, but his Colt was missing. Lee plunged ahead into the forest depths, weaving his way wildly through the spruce and cedars, hearing voices behind him and the sounds of pursuit.

He ran on, his lungs burning. Twice he stumbled over unseen obstacles as his clouded vision failed to discern a rock or tree root. He ran on, ran with his heart pounding against his ribcage, an angry vulture trying to free itself. His eyes were filled with blood and his lungs seemed to have lost their capacity. Reaching the edge of a stony ledge he failed to stop in time and found himself hurtling through space before he jolted harshly against the solid earth below and fell into utter insentient blackness.

FIVE

Now what? Calvin Manassas was regretting the day he had set eyes on this hunting party. He sat down on a nearby boulder, the yellow hound, Jack, at his boots and gazed briefly at the high reaches of the mountains. He wiped his eyes, ruffled his graying hair and looked upslope and down. Lee's old cabin had been empty when Calvin had finally reached it; the woman, Lucinda, was nowhere to be seen. He wondered if she could have made her way back to the wagon camp without his having seen her, but knew that was almost impossible.

Then where had she gone? Dressed as she was, shod as she was, as unfamiliar as she was with the wild country, if she had gone on foot into the mile upon mile of forest, she had effectively committed suicide. She would fall from the heights or freeze or starve and herself be eaten by the wild creatures.

Now what? Manassas thought again.

He had promised Lee that he would see that the woman got downriver to Rock Springs. There she would be able to make stagecoach connections to the East. To that end Lee had given him $500 in gold to hand over to Lucinda to start her on her way. Well, Manassas had the gold in a chamois pouch he carried attached to a rawhide string tied around his neck.

But he did not have the woman!

How far would Lee want him to go . . . no, how far must he go? Calvin shook his head, knowing that no matter what he could not leave a city woman alone out here. She likely did not even know which direction she meant to go. And she did not have a chance of making it to Rock Springs if she did.

'Jack,' Manassas said to the hound which got up eagerly as his master spoke – something momentous, exciting, was in the wind – 'we got to do some tracking.' Manassas got to his feet and took up the reins to his saddle horse which stood tethered behind the wagon he had driven to Lee's parcel.

It was then that he heard a fusillade of shots in the near distance. Fifty shots, a hundred. It echoed like his memories of Bull Run. There was killing, much killing afoot. And Manassas knew from the direction what had happened. He swung into the saddle of his horse, his eyes narrow, his face grim.

He wanted to rush to Lee's aid, but if what he believed to have happened was what had actually occurred, Lee would have been the first man to go down. They would have had to kill him.

'Come on, dog,' Manassas growled at Jack. It was a cruel day although the sunlight shone brilliantly through the dark reaches of the pines. A cruel and savage day. Somehow it made Manassas more determined to find Lucinda. What had he and Lee discussed? No matter if she truly was a madwoman, she deserved better than to be living with these savages she traveled among.

Which way? Was there a way? Was there an up and down, a north or south? Lucinda dragged herself through a screen of brittle manzanita which snagged her dress with each effort. She lifted her eyes to the timber beyond the tangled brush, willing herself to be there. Why did one feel so sheltered in the forest. This was agony. The line of travel had seemed easier, but had proven to be much more difficult. Now she was tugged back again by the reddish branches of the manzanita, and the gray shale that littered the steep slope slashed at her knees and elbows once more as she fell.

She remained against the cold earth, crying soundlessly into her upraised arm. What had happened to her life? Where was she going in this hell-land? Why had they brought her here! She heard the smallest sound, a tiny scuffling sound, and then the faint but clear fall of pebbles and trickling sand. She raised her deep blue eyes uncertainly and peered into the emptiness surrounding her. A wild animal? Indians moving toward her? She waited, listening cautiously and then started on, afraid to remain where she was, on that tangled hillside.

She crawled now like an animal, her hair a tangle, blood on her shoulders, knees, feet and hands. She crept toward a low ridge and lifted her head just enough to see over it. And there below, in a small landslide fallen to the base of the escarpment, she saw a man. He was alive, but he had no strength in his limbs. His arms raised as if they had no more sinew than a marionette's. He mewled like a child.

Lucinda started down the rocky slope toward him. As her shadow crossed his face, he spoke.

'Can you help me to dig out from under these rocks?' Lee Trent asked.

Lucinda began digging at the stones the landslide had brought tumbling down to cover Lee's body. She broke her fingernails and sprained a wrist, but she worked earnestly, biting at her lower lip in intense concentration. Lee was finally able to drag himself free from the mound of sand and rocks and pull himself to the foot of the bluff where he propped his back against the wall of the canyon and breathed slowly, deeply, his eyes closed. His leg hurt; there was blood in his eyes and a constant heavy thudding at the base of his skull.

'Thanks,' he said with a narrow smile. 'Where did you come from, Lucinda?'

'When I woke up this morning,' she said, sitting beside him, 'you were gone. I didn't know what to do. Then I saw some of the Texans searching the woods. There's a man called Pawnee . . . he's frightening. Terrible.' She shuddered, 'I saw that everyone had traveled on except for this small bunch of men. I knew I had to run, but I had no idea where to go. I got lost and I've been hiding and running since.'

'It's my fault,' Lee said, closing his eyes heavily. 'I thought I had things taken care of for you. I guess Manassas couldn't get back early enough from his place.'

'You?' Lucinda asked with her blue sapphire eyes on his, searching them. 'What happened to you?'

'Didn't you hear the guns?' Lee asked.

'Guns?' she asked perplexed. 'Oh, dear God! I thought it was distant thunder. Now I remember

81

– when we were on the buffalo plains and all the men began firing their guns wantonly. They would have taken the entire herd if their barrels hadn't got too hot. The sky was filled with acrid black smoke. It was the same sound. . . .'

'It was the same sound.'

'Then he has taken his forst elk,' Lucinda said, nodding heavily. 'Now he has only to complete the second part of his plan and they will go home satisfied.'

Lee watched the girl. He stretched his arm carefully and winced with pain; something had happened to his elbow. He leaned his head back against the shaded sandy bluff, and then it came to him. It couldn't be what he had imagined. Without meaning to, he forcefully took Lucinda's shoulders and shook her.

'The second part of his plan! Lucinda, tell me what you mean.'

She was so startled that she opened her mouth as if she would scream, but she did not. Lee loosened his grip on her shoulders and let his hands fall away as he waited. He knew what she was going to say somehow. Knew but could not assimilate the idea.

She looked to the ragged line of pines atop the ridge and then back to him. 'I believed that you knew. I thought you understood that that was why he paid you so much money, Lee. It wasn't the wapiti that he wanted to hunt to decorate his hunting lodge. He has come hunting another trophy. A Great Elk, indeed, but not the one you called Ulysses.'

Lee groaned and buried his head in his one good hand. 'I should have . . . are you sure, Lucinda?'

'Or am I mad?' she asked with a bittersweet smile. 'Yes, Lee, I am sure. They have talked of nothing else for weeks. They want as a trophy, an Indian chief in full regalia. It will be a challenge for his taxidermist, so the baron says.'

Lee was unable to speak. He could not believe the savagery this implied. As angry as he was, as confused and injured as he was, it suddenly became clear to him what they wanted: 'Great Elk!' Four Dove's father. The man who had treated him like a son, given him the parcel where he now lived in peace, a trusted and valued friend. 'Good God,' Lee said mournfully. 'What have I brought upon the land.'

'Didn't you wonder?' Lucinda asked quietly. She took his rough hand and held it on her lap. 'Didn't you wonder why there are so many men in the party? Why they kept me locked away so that I might not slip and give away their plan? Why they were so interested in your 'parcel' specifically as a hunting site.'

'It's barbaric,' Lee said between compressed

lips. He could find no stronger word for his feelings. He repeated it.

'What will you do?' Lucinda asked, and her hand applied a slight pressure to Lee's. 'What can we do?' She shook her head. 'You don't know me. My background. My upbringing. My family's problems concerning the duke, but I am not a woman to countenance this mad endeavor they have formulated, and—' She halted and Lee prompted her.

'And, Lee, I know one other thing – the duke covets your land, and he fully intends for you to be done away with one way or the other.'

'By him . . .' Lee said growing disconsolate, 'or by the Cheyenne if they believe I have broken their trust.'

'Yes. You see,' Lucinda went on, 'they may be crazy and they are barbaric, but they are not fools.'

'*Hey*!' The voice echoed down the rocky valley, bringing their heads up in unison. Manassas, followed as always by Jack, rode his horse carefully down the rough wash toward them. 'Here I am out riding in the sun and you two are sitting here holding hands.'

Lucinda jerked her hand away. Lee rose painfully, knowing that Manassas' words only conveyed relief at finding them both alive.

'It took you long enough,' Lee said, rising to greet Calvin Manassas as he swung down stiffly from his horse. Jack rushed to greet Lee, always happy to run across an old friend. He snuffled warily at Lucinda. He knew that he should remember her, but was not quite sure if she was friend or foe.

'I'd've been here sooner,' Calvin answered, 'except this lady cuts a mean trail. Just when I thought I had her, she took to the shale slopes – and on all fours. It was like tracking an Apache!' Growing serious, he asked, 'Was what I thought I heard – what happened, Lee?'

'They must have slaughtered a quarter of the herd, Calvin. Maybe thirty, forty wapiti.'

'So I thought, so I thought,' the old mountain man said sadly. He continued to glance at Lucinda from time to time, wondering exactly how she fit into the picture. Well, maybe Lee would tell him later, maybe not. For now. . . .

'What are we going to do, Lee?' Manassas asked.

'We've got to get to Great Elk's camp to tell him of the danger,' Lee said.

'He'll be disappointed in you, Lee,' Calvin said.

'Yes. Probably. But, Cal, he'll be alive.'

'Any conflict,' Manassas said with a heavy tone, 'and the army will be up here. They'll take the baron's word against that of an Indian. It might

85

mean the end of the Green River band of Cheyenne. And of you, Lee,' he added.

'I've already resigned myself to that, Cal,' Lee replied. His eyes briefly surveyed the high reaches of the Wapiti Range. 'Even if we're successful in stopping this, Great Elk still will never have faith in me again for bringing these killers onto the parcel. If we fail, well, the army will likely evict the Cheyenne and place them on a reservation. Unless I totally miss my guess – from what Lucinda has told me – the duke has probably already filed for property rights on the parcel.'

'It was my understanding,' Lucinda told them, 'although they seldom spoke in front of me, that the elk were to be killed or driven from the land and Texas cattle brought onto the rich grass.'

'I can see that,' Lee said sadly. 'It would mean a huge profit if cattle were installed here. What it means to the wild animals . . . it would be nothing short of extermination.'

'This is all my fault, Lee,' Manassas said with a deeply apologetic tone. 'I wanted to make fifty lousy dollars. Greedy fool that I was.'

'It wasn't your fault,' Lee assured him. 'It's the times, Calvin. Things change and old loners like us can't do much about it. No matter,' he said with strength, 'as long as there's a bit of wild country left, I'll be upon it. The Cheyenne, however . . . they may not have that choice, Cal.'

They made their way through the pines, following the narrow winding trails. It was the long way around, but neither of the men had the inclination to go by way of the valley where the slaughter had been done. Even if the baron and all of his men had gone, it was something they did not wish to see.

The trees loomed large and dark pointing to a shifting gray sky where shelves of clouds gathered above the peaks. A single crow circled high against the clouds and Lee glanced at it, knowing it would not be long now before the sky above the valley of the wapiti would be stained black by the cloud of vultures which were sure to gather.

Lucinda clung wearily to the saddlehorn, her body weaving from side to side. And now and then she would ask how much further they had to go before she could dismount. They had crossed the thin trickle of the icy rill bisecting the flats when she suddenly made a small whimpering sound and pitched headfirst from the saddle.

Lee was barely able to catch her and the pain it caused his torn arm was immense. He knelt with her, looking down at her pale scratched face.

'Think we can get her back in the saddle?' Manassas asked with concern.

'We'd better not try,' Lee replied, looking up. 'It's no more than a half-mile to the Cheyenne camp. I'll carry her.'

'Lee . . .' Calvin asked uncertainly. 'Are you sure you can?'

'We'll make it,' Lee assured him with a confidence he did not feel. 'You ride awhile, Calvin.'

Calvin began to argue, but even to him his arguments made no sense. He knew he couldn't carry the woman and his own legs were weary with the trudging uphill and down which had brought them to the border of the Cheyenne land. Nodding, he swung tiredly aboard the dun and they started on through the trees, now fewer and scattered.

Finally, with Lee laboring under Lucinda's weight, they crested a rocky ridge decorated only by a single mammoth pine, wind-twisted and lightning-struck, and looked down upon the Cheyenne encampment. Long rows of tepees stretched out in a spoke pattern from the dwelling of the chief and smoke rose from a dozen cookfires. Children played and two braves raced their spotted ponies in the distance to the cheers of other men. Lee filled his lungs, and glanced at Manassas.

'Let's go on down, Calvin.'

They had gone no more than a hundred yards down the grassy slope toward the village before the camp dogs began to yap and people stopped to turn toward them, shading their eyes to watch the arriving strangers. Half-a-dozen young braves mounted their ponies and snatched up lances or rifles and advanced toward them in a scowling rank.

One of the young warriors howled a fierce warning, but Lee saw another brave reach out a restraining hand and peer at them with narrowed eyes. Weapons were lowered as Lee, struggling on with the woman in black in his arms, approached. Women, children, old men gathered to watch and parted to allow the ragged party to pass. Camp dogs growled at Jack and sniffed the intruder. Jack's hackles rose, but he did not bite and they skulked away, leaving the yellow hound alone.

The largest tent belonged to Great Elk. It was painted with symbols of bears and buffalo, long winter hunts and fierce battles. Lee, barely able to walk, approached it with Manassas at his side. The great chief emerged suddenly from the teepee, his white hair worn loose, falling across his shoulders. His bare chest was decorated with a bear claw necklace. He watched the approaching party without expression. As Lee stumbled to the entrance to his teepee, Great Elk nodded and stepped aside, allowing Lee to enter.

Lee made it to the bed in the corner where

piled furs and blankets made a magnificently soft and warm sleeping place. He managed to place Lucinda down on the bed before heavy shadows began to fill in the space behind his eyes and without speaking, he fell to the floor, unconscious.

He could not tell how long he slept. Great Elk was not there when he opened his eyes again, nor was Manassas. Embers burned low in the fire ring and he watched with fascination as lazy curlicues rose toward the smoke hole overhead. For a very long time he tried to remember where he was, how he had come to be here, what had happened.

Sitting halfway up his head thudded with torment and he remained where he was, hands limply dangling, head hanging between his knees.

Now who. . . ? Then he recognized Lucinda, sleeping on the bed and recalled a part of what had happened. She seemed deeply asleep; but it also seemed to be a pained, troubled sleep, which was no surprise considering what she had been through.

Lee told himself to rise, willed his body to obey his commands, but he continued to sit as he was, unstirring. He felt a breath of cool air enter the teepee and sensed rather than saw that it was dark outside. Someone had come in, and he lifted his

90

eyes to see who it was.

'And so,' Four Dove said to him. 'You are still the same man, Lee Trent. Go find young women to rescue and take them home with you!'

SIX

The slender young woman did not resemble the Four Dove that Lee remembered, and yet she did. She was taller, of course, her figure fuller. She wore a white, fringed elkskin dress with beaded bodice. Her face was stern, but there was a sort of mocking laughter in the depths of her eyes. Lee struggled to get to his feet, but could not manage it. Four Dove went to her knees beside him.

'It is you, Lee Trent,' she said, lifting his chin to study his battered face.

'Yes. And it is you, Four Dove.' He shook his head. 'I cannot believe what a difference four years can make. You were just a girl!'

But no longer, he thought. Now she was a self-confident, handsome woman. Her dark hair hung in a single braid down her back. She had scooted to the fire ring and begun heating water. 'You are filthy, Lee. What has happened?'

'Some men came upon my land . . . I'll tell you all about it later. When your father is here as well.' They settled into silent remembrances while the water she placed on the fire to heat boiled. She found a strip of clean cloth and began cleaning his face with small intakes of breath. 'Your arm hurts – I can see by the way you move.'

'Yes. It's not broken, but only twisted.' He watched her as she dabbed at his cuts, her movements as lithe as a cat's, her face serious. He could not fail to notice her eyes, black as night, intense, and from time to time flickering to the bed where Lucinda lay.

'She is your woman, this one?' Four Dove asked abruptly, sitting back. Lee smiled.

'No. The men who came had her held prisoner. Manassas and I planned to set her free and help her get home.'

'I see,' Four Dove answered with severe softness. 'Remove your shirt, Lee Trent. I can tell that you have been badly beaten.'

'Actually,' he admitted, 'I fell off a cliff!'

He thought the remark would draw a laugh from Four Dove, but she only replied, 'It is the same thing.'

'Do you have the time to tend me?' Lee asked, unbuttoning his shirt.

'I have the time,' Four Dove said, wringing the cloth out in the pot. 'Why would I not have the time to aid the man who once rescued me?'

'That was so long ago. . . .'

'Gratitude has a long memory,' she said. Four Dove sat near to him, working on his scratches and bruises. Her breath was intent and warm.

'I'm sorry,' Lee said. His hand barely brushed hers as he spoke. 'I only thought that maybe you should be home . . . taking care of your husband and your family.'

She did not seem to hear him. She had found the open wound on his back. 'This will require a poultice. I will see to it.' Then she held the cloth to the back of his neck where he had been clubbed down. Her touch was soothing. She was inches from him. Her mouth was still set; only her eyes smiled.

'I have no family, Lee Trent,' Four Dove said in a ragged whisper. 'I have no children. Do you not remember what I told you long ago?'

'A child's utterance,' Lee said uneasily.

'Yes. And now I am a woman who has waited through the years for you. What was it I said, Lee?' she prompted.

'I don't remember,' he lied, as she leaned even nearer.

'I told you, "My name is Four Dove, and you are my man".'

The smoke continued to rise in lazy blue ribbons. Four Dove's hand had fallen away and she now rested on her knees studying him. 'Had you forgotten that?' she asked.

'You were a child only, Four Dove. You had some romantic dream . . .'

'All of life is a series of dreams. If you knew how often I have come onto your parcel to watch you at work, chopping wood, mowing hay . . . resting alone in the pine shadows when you became weary. . . .'

'Lee Trent!' the flap to the teepee was flung open and Great Elk entered. He was obviously not pleased, but it was not the sight of his daughter nursing him that angered him. Four Dove did not move nor so much as glance back at her father. Manassas had slipped in silently and removed himself to one side of the huge tent.

'My friend,' Lee said, struggling to rise to his feet. Great Elk gestured.

'Stay down. I know you have been injured.' The Cheyenne chief came near to the flickering fire and folded his arms. His face was grim and his eyes dark with suppressed anger. 'Why have you brought these white men onto our land! I rose with the morning and walked out beneath the pleasing sky and before an hour had passed we heard from our camp the roar of a hundred guns. I sent two swift scouts on their ponies to discover the cause of it all and they came back to tell me sadly that dozens of white hunters had slaughtered a herd of wapiti. Left the meat and the hides on the ground, left the crippled to die. That the great stag had been killed and his antlers ripped from his head.' His fury was evident.

'If we may speak,' Lee said in a conciliatory voice, gesturing for the chief to sit down near him. 'You are my father and my brother, my friend. What has happened has occurred because of trickery, not because I willed it so.'

'Most of it is my fault,' Manassas said, and Great Elk spared him one hostile curious glance.

'Let me explain,' Lee said. 'If you will be patient with me, my Father, I will tell you what has happened.'

Doubtfully, still angry, Great Elk lifted one hand in command and Four Dove scrambled to her feet to go to the small cedar chest among the chief's possessions and return with his red clay pipe. Sitting again beside Lee she handed the pipe dutifully to her father who began to smoke as Lee related all he knew of what had occurred.

Great Elk could not speak for a long while. His eyes remained fixed on Lee's. Out of the corner of his eye he saw that Lucinda had awakened; she sat up and rubbed her arms, one of which was bare because her dress had been torn. Her eyes were glazed. Now she looked around her in aston-ishment.

'Four Dove,' the Cheyenne chief said, 'take this

woman and clean her wounds. Feed her and find her clean clothes while I talk to Lee.'

Four Dove looked at the dazed European woman, her mouth set. For a moment Lee thought Four Dove was not going to do it, but her father's command had been firm. Lucinda looked at Lee, her sapphire eyes questioning.

'Lee?'

'It's all right, Lucinda. These people are my friends.'

'Can you get up, woman?' Four Dove asked. At Lucinda's weak nod, the Cheyenne woman said, 'Good, then do so. Come with me to the women's tent.' As Lucinda rose unsteadily Four Dove glared contemptuously at her and at Lee.

'Don't worry, Lucinda,' Lee Trent said, smiling at the uncertain woman. 'It will be all right.'

After the two women had departed, Great Elk relit his clay pipe and said in a tight voice, 'This is very bad, Lee Trent. This trouble that you have brought onto our land.'

'I told you it was mostly my—' Manassas began, but Lee silenced him with a small gesture. It was Great Elk's turn to speak, and to interrupt the chief was a serious breach of etiquette.

'What is it they want?' Great Elk asked Lee.

'My parcel' – his brown eyes lifted to Great Elk's – 'and your land as well, I believe.'

'The white president has signed a letter that

gives us this land forever,' Great Elk said with fervor. 'He sent me a medallion of bronze along with this letter! Shall I show it to you?'

'I have seen it, Great Elk,' Lee said in a quieter voice.

'Well, then. . . .' Great Elk spread his hands. 'These whites must honor that treaty.'

'The only way to make them honor it would be to send for the soldiers,' Lee believed.

'No! Never will the horse soldiers come upon my land.'

'I know how you feel, Great Elk,' Lee responded, looking across the camp-fire into the Cheyenne's eyes. 'But I believe that the strangers mean to lure the army into this anyway. I believe that they intend to start a war. I believe they mean to kill you and whoever gets in their way and then tell the army that your people attacked them.'

'That cannot be!' Great Elk said in a fury strong enough to bring him to his feet. 'No men are so treacherous, so greedy.'

'What can we do, Lee Trent?' the chief asked after a long pause when Lee was sure thoughts of bloody vengeance drifted through his mind – that, of course, would only be fulfilling the wishes of the strangers. Great Elk spread his strong hands.

'We will formulate a plan,' Lee said. 'Perhaps

we should reconsider notifying the army ourselves.'

'No!' Great Elk's voice was definite. 'Once the army comes upon Indian land, the Indian must leave or become a slave upon it. Then, people like these men – others, if not them, will come in, raise beef to sell to the army, become rich and powerful . . . and the elk will be gone, none left even to hunt for our winter meals.

'It is always the same,' Great Elk said, not without cause, 'we shall become wanderers upon our own land again.'

'All right,' Lee said, agreeing with the Cheyenne despite himself. 'We must think this through, discuss it. 'There is always a way if men of good faith work together.'

Beyond the tent a warrior cried out and Great Elk, expecting the worst, slipped out of the teepee flap, followed by Lee and Manassas. Ten or twelve braves came running with weapons in their hands as Lee peered into the purple twilight at the incoming rider. Recognizing him, he told the Cheyenne.

'It's all right, Great Elk,' Lee said.

'It is a friend of yours?' the Cheyenne asked.

'I'm not quite sure,' Lee said honestly, and the three waited, watching Darby Pierce riding cautiously toward the camp, leading Shoshone.

Later, after the Cheyenne and his guests had

eaten, served by the silent woman inside the fire-lit teepee, Pierce told them what had happened to him. There was a sadness drawing down the corners of the mouth of the blond man from Baltimore now. The dancing of the low flames etched shadows on his face.

'I had gone out again to look for Lucinda as you and the hunting party rolled out of camp. I really had no idea where to look, but I needed to be doing *something* to try to help her, knowing what rough country this is.

'I hadn't been out for more than an hour,' he continued, 'before I heard great volleys of gunfire. It sounded like a pitched battle. I thought – forgive me, sir,' he said to Great Elk, 'I know little of your ways and of this country, and my first thought was that a war party of Indians had attacked the hunters. I rode that way using spurs and quirt both.

'By the time I got there it was all over, of course. It was . . .' Pierce paused, looking for the right words, 'ghastly,' he concluded. 'I've never seen such wanton butchery.' Darby Pierce was silent again for a little while, lost in unhappy reverie.

'Of course as soon as I saw it, I knew what had happened, knew that the Indians weren't involved.'

'Thank you,' Great Elk said with a chill in his tone.

'I apologize, sir – as I say, I am new in this country. Immediately,' he said to Lee Trent, 'I knew I had to find safety somewhere, but I had no idea where to go. I knew there was an Indian encampment somewhere around, and you had said they were friends of yours. Scanning the skies I could make out camp-fires as the day began to grow cool. I was frightened, frankly, to try seeking shelter here, but as I said, there was nowhere else to go.

'As I entered the pines again, to try finding my way here under cover, I heard a horse whickering. A little further on I saw your red roan with its distinctive splash of white on its flank. I found Shoshone looking down from a rocky bluff. I looked over, but there was no one down there.'

Lee said, 'Lucinda and Manassas had already found me.'

'I see,' Pierce said. 'Well, there was Shoshone, either trying to find a way down the cliff or waiting for you to return. I had the devil of a time getting him to let me lead him, but after a while he acquiesced. Maybe as he drew nearer he knew where we were going.'

Pierce shrugged. 'So here I am. That's my sad little story in short. The only thing I regret is not having found Lucinda. Of course I'm going back over there in the morning.'

At that moment the two women entered Great

Elk's teepee. They hesitated, standing side by side at the tent entrance for a moment. Pierce gaped at Lucinda and a pretty young Indian woman. Both of the same slender build, both with raven dark hair and both wearing bleached, fringed elkskin dresses. They might have been sisters except for Lucinda's lighter skin and those startling blue eyes.

Lee got to his feet to welcome Four Dove and Lucinda. Manassas looked from one woman to the other, hardly believing his eyes, so alike were they, and he came to an understanding of the odd questions Lee had put to him earlier. For, looking at the two girls, it seemed that the same thing had indeed happened twice to Lee Trent.

'Are you through with talk for the evening, Father?' Four Dove asked, letting her eyes shuttle briefly to Lee's.

'Yes,' Great Elk answered. 'This must be slept upon. I do not trust myself to make hasty answer to so serious a problem. I must sleep.' He did indeed look strained. Great problems can line a face and weary one. Great Elk, by firelight, looked more near his real age. Which was. . .? Lee didn't know. But the old stag was worn down by concerns and age rode him heavily at this moment.

'Sleep, then, Father,' Four Dove said. 'I shall clean away your bowls and cups.'

She then began to clean up after their meal as Great Elk went to his bed with careful steps, the gait of a man who has grown suddenly weary. When Lee glanced away from the great chief, he saw to his surprise that Lucinda was assisting Four Dove in her work. It was incredible to see the pampered noblewoman chip in like that. But then, Lee reflected, he did not know much about Lucinda at all. She had proved to be nothing like he had imagined her to be before their meeting.

For that matter, neither was Darby Pierce what they had first imagined him to be. What the young Easterner had done took quite a bit of courage.

The three visiting men were given a teepee of their own in which to sleep.

Stretched out on their blankets, none could fall asleep. Lee, nagged by his injuries had the worst time of it. Pierce and Manassas were uneasy, realizing fully that the worst had not yet occurred. Somewhere out there in the night Baron Stromberg was plotting against the Indians as well as Lee, Calvin, and the traitor Darby Pierce. The duke would be fuming. His promised bride had gone missing. He still had no firm grip on his new 'duchy', that was Lee Trent's parcel. Pierce lay awake trying to figure out their strategy, wondering at their machinations. What had the arrangement between Stromberg and the duke been?

103

Obviously their agreement with his father had been a sham. Had the elder Pierce been led to provision this excursion in hopes of securing a lucrative contract? That could very well be, Darby thought, looking back. His father had been nearly desperate. Any condition might have seemed a strengthening of the agreement.

The hunters' plan, taken down to its basics, was simple and showed dark imagination. Engage the Cheyenne in a war against the whites, have the Indians driven from the land, assume Lee's parcel for cattle to be driven up from Texas, presumably by men they had made contact with through John Saturday. Beyond that . . . it was tiring to keep thinking of it, but Darby could not sleep.

He was not alone. He saw a match spark, saw Manassas sitting up on his blanket, light his pipe.

'What now, Lee?' the old man asked.

Trent was on his blanket, hands behind his head. 'What's your thinking, Calvin?' Lee asked in return.

'Well, sir,' Manassas said, 'truth be told, I haven't got a good idea. I know that we can't involve the Cheyenne. It would do great harm to them, maybe life on a reservation, certainly loss of their land. And,' Manassas said, belatedly waving out his burning match, 'we can't have the soldiers involved. Great Elk won't hear of it. We'll never be able to convince him that it's a good idea to have bluecoats swarming over his country.'

'You're right, of course,' Lee said thoughtfully. 'That cuts short our options, doesn't it.'

'Like the man trying to make a one-ended rope,' Manassas said wearily.

Darby didn't know that one. 'What do you mean?' he asked.

'You know how you do that,' Manassas said. 'You take a regular two-ended rope and cut one end off.'

Darby Pierce smiled, but only faintly. He got Calvin's meaning. No matter what they did it was going to have the same result. A bad one.

'We have no options,' Lee said from the deep shadows. 'We can't let the Cheyenne get involved. We can't call in the soldiers.' They heard him shift his position, saw him sit up in his bed and reach for his hat.

'And so?' Darby asked.

'And so, son, we take care of this by ourselves.' Lee rose then and slipped out of the tent into the star-shadowed night. Darby Pierce looked after him as the tent flap closed and the teepee grew dark again except for the faint red glow of Calvin's pipe.

'He was kidding, right?' the man from Baltimore asked. 'I mean ... it can't be done! The three of us against the baron's army?'

Manassas was slow in answering. He put out his

pipe, smothering the coal with his thumb and stretched out again on his blankets. When he spoke it was in a soft, fine voice.

'Darby – Lee Trent isn't given to idle statements. He wouldn't joke about a thing like this. If he said it, he means to try it. And if he says it,' the old man said with a throaty chuckle, 'I wouldn't lay odds against it. You'd have to know the man.'

Lee walked the camp, smelling the fading cookfires, hearing only the quiet sounds of people bedding down. The stars were gleaming silver in a blue-black sky. From somewhere Jack, the yellow hound, had emerged to find him and follow along, giving his attention to shadows where the camp dogs might be lying in wait.

She met him at the edge of the camp, not far from where the oak grove began and the river flowed gently past.

'Hello, Four Dove,' he said, as the woman walked slowly toward him, her hands clasped behind her back. They continued on their way and after a minute the Cheyenne woman hooked her hand around his arm.

'Do you think I am foolish, Lee Trent?'

'I don't know. I think everyone is foolish at times,' he said, as he halted near enough to see the silver stream running beyond the great oaks. She looked up at his strong profile, lifted a pleading hand and let it fall again. There was starlight in her eyes and he knew by the scent that she had freshly washed and brushed her hair which now fell loose across her shoulders like a raven-black waterfall.

'I mean,' she went on with a sort of impatient vigor, 'saying that I still love you after all these years have passed.'

Lee turned her shoulders so that she faced him and he smiled. His eyes, she saw, were distant and concerned. 'I believe that you think it is so. It is the greatest compliment anyone has ever paid me, Four Dove.'

'But you do not love me!' she said with restrained emotions. 'Is it this other woman?' her eyes turned down and Lee lifted her chin with his thumb. He shook his head and his smile became more real, yet sadder.

'I don't know that woman, Four Dove. Not at all.'

'Lee . . .' she pleaded.

'Nor do I know you, Four Dove. I did not know the child you were; I don't know the woman you have become.'

'Lee Trent,' Four Dove answered, 'You do not need to know anything about me. I love you: that is all you need to know.'

And for that moment, on that night, he did believe her.

SEVEN

Darby Pierce didn't know if Lee Trent had arisen early or had been awake all night. But as he himself opened his tired eyes and swung around on his blankets, there Lee Trent was surveying him, his face haggard. Dawn was breaking outside – the low complaints of dogs mingled with the muted morning conversations of men and women in the Cheyenne camp. Once, as Darby tried to pry the sleep from his eyes, a young boy – perhaps on a dare – peered into the teepee and then ran away, allowing him a brief glimpse of the orange skies and of the deep-green forested hills.

Manassas sat near Lee Trent, puffing at his constant companion, his stubby pipe. Jack the dog rose and licked Darby's hand in a lazy welcome. Darby looked at Lee and sensing that the man had something to say, asked, 'Well?'

'Good morning,' Lee said.

'Good morning,' Darby said with an irritation he could not define. 'What is it, then?'

'Manassas and I have been talking,' Lee told the blond-haired Easterner. 'We think you ought to head home.'

'Do you?' Pierce asked stiffly.

'Yes,' Lee told him. 'And here's why—'

'Because you're going to fight the baron and his crew and you think I'd be no help at all!' Darby finished for him.

'I didn't say that.'

'You don't know the lay of the land,' Manassas said.

'Neither do they,' Darby said stubbornly. 'What do you want me to do, cut and run? Ride two thousand miles home, leaving you two in the lurch. Well, blast you, I'm not going. I've as big a score to settle with the baron as you have.' His words were definite and neither of the two mountain men responded. They had offered him a way out; if he was man enough to stay, then they could not refuse. There was no denying the fact that they needed as many guns as they could muster. Darby thought he saw Lee smile thinly, but the light was poor inside the teepee, and he could not be sure.

With full daylight's arrival, Lee walked heavily across the camp to Great Elk's teepee. Calling first, he was summoned inside to find the

Cheyenne chief sitting meditatively over a low-burning fire. Four Dove sat across the large tent, repairing a pair of moccasins. Their eyes met only briefly, but Great Elk caught the meaningful glances.

'Sit down, Lee Trent,' Great Elk said and Lee lowered himself stiffly. The battering his body had taken would require many days to heal. 'You have had the night to contemplate, Lee; what did your dreams tell you?'

Lee leaned forward intently, his hands clasped together. 'That you are correct about not allowing soldiers onto your land; that I am correct that the Cheyenne must not engage in a battle.'

'Who, then, is there to wage war?' Great Elk asked. Lee told him simply.

'Me.'

'So – I see. Lee, can you kill your own kind?'

'What do you mean, Father?'

'These men are also whites – you invited them upon your land.'

'These men are far from being my friends.'

'They are white,' Great Elk insisted.

'Surely you remember the great war in the East when whites fought whites.' Great Elk nodded, unconvinced. 'Men fought their own brothers, Great Elk. But that was for a cause. These people from across the great sea are not even known to me.'

110

'They are whites,' Great Elk repeated with bitter caution.

'And so!' Lee grew a little heated. 'The Shoshone are Indians. Can you tell me that you love the Shoshones because of that? Would you fight on the side of the Shoshones?'

'You know I would not.'

'Then put those thoughts aside, Father. I fight for you – and for myself. I would never betray you. If you like I will now return my rights to the parcel and leave this country.'

'And I will go with him,' Four Dove said, putting her sewing aside. She rose from her work, holding her head proudly.

'You . . .' Great Elk could make no answer. He looked from his daughter to Lee and back again. 'Leave us alone, Four Dove! You speak foolishly.'

Four Dove nodded her obedience, but as she passed Lee she let her hand trail across his shoulder. Then she swept out into the brilliant sunlight. Lee said nothing of the moment.

'We can't allow your people to take up arms against these strangers,' Lee said intensely. 'I ask you to either move your camp a little . . .'

'I will not be pushed from my chosen site!' Great Elk said angrily.

'Very well, then. I thought not. In that case, you must keep yourself hidden, Great Elk.'

The Cheyenne chief was too angry to respond

for a minute, then he rumbled, 'I hide away from no men. I am no coward, Lee Trent.'

'No,' Lee said, trying to pacify the old warrior. 'Great Elk, I ask you – what would you call a man who stood in front of a thousand stampeding buffalo? Brave? Or only a fool?'

'I do not understand you.'

'I think you do. Great Elk, these men mean to kill you. What would your braves do if that happened?'

'There would be no holding them back. They would ride to avenge my death.'

'Yes! And then the soldiers would certainly come.'

'Still, I say let a man among them try his hand at murdering me,' the Cheyenne said challengingly.

'They won't do it that way, don't you see? Great Elk,' Lee said more intently, his eyes searching those of the Indian chief. 'They have guns that can kill a man from a mile away! They know how to use them, and they do not miss. I have watched them. You would not even see the smoke from the rifle. That is why they have brought these weapons west.' He held up a hand so that Great Elk would not interrupt him.

'They have been heard bragging about how they would kill you and skin you. I believe that part of the boast was a cruel exaggeration to frighten and impress the young woman I arrived here with, but the intention behind the savage promise is valid enough. They mean to kill you and, once that is done, your people will be dragged inexorably into the conflict. They will be mad to extract revenge for your death.'

'I see.' Great Elk pondered everything Lee Trent had said for a long while. He shook his head gravely, liking none of what he had heard.

'I can only ask you, Great Elk, to be prudent and restrain yourself – for the good of your people.'

'What did Great Elk think of the way you spun it out to him?' Manassas asked as Lee met him near the brush corral where their horses had been kept.

'Not much,' Lee said glumly.

'I didn't think so. A warrior's pride is involved here, Lee. No Cheyenne is going to like the idea of appearing to be a coward.'

'I know. Calvin, that only means we have to do our work – successfully – before Great Elk can brood too long on the matter.'

'Do you still have those ideas percolating in your mind?' Manassas asked, throwing the saddle onto his dun horse's back. 'About how we're going to defeat that army the baron has, I mean.'

'Oh that,' Lee said, untying Shoshone, smoothing his saddle blanket, 'I never had any ideas at all.'

'I didn't think so,' Calvin said dryly. He leaned his back against his horse as he fished for and lit his pipe. 'But – it seems about the right time, don't it, Lee, to come up with some?'

Calvin indicated an approaching figure with a nod of his head and Lee shifted his eyes to watch a grim-faced Darby Pierce walking toward the pen, his eyes cast down. 'Think we ought to tell him what good generals we aren't?'

'Probably not just now,' Lee said. 'Besides, maybe we're smarter than we think, Calvin.'

'I hope so! You're the boss, Lee. Maybe you *can* show us how to make a one-ended rope. There's another that has too much faith in you, General,' the old mountain man said, and Lee looked in the indicated direction to see Four Dove watching them saddle their ponies.

From the unmarried women's tent then, they watched as Lucinda rushed to Four Dove. She lifted a hand toward the departing men and said something they could not hear. Her eyes were fixed on Darby Pierce. Four Dove, with her eyes still on Lee, turned the European woman whose face was buried in her hands and led her away, her arm across the sobbing woman's shoulder.

Darby Pierce had halted in his steps and stood watching the two women until they had ducked

114

inside the teepee and could be seen no more. Manassas nudged Lee with his elbow, but Lee did not smile.

'Well,' Manassas said as Pierce arrived. 'It seems the lady has taken a shine to you.'

'Shut up!' Darby said roughly. This was so far from his usual manner that Calvin made an apologetic gesture and returned to his horse, swinging aboard.

'Well?' Lee asked.

'She's far too good for me.'

'No one's too good for anybody. What does she say . . . about the two of you?' Lee asked.

'Nothing. We never spoke of it.'

'Because . . .'

'Because she was betrothed to the duke, Lee. Damnit, you knew that! I'm not a cad.'

'And because you have a sweetheart back home?'

Pierce turned his back, tightening the cinches of the saddle on his own horse. 'I just told you that because . . . well, Lee, the lady sent me a letter a month ago. I got it in Kansas City.' He smiled bitterly, weakly. 'She's found another man. One whose father has money, one who doesn't ride out to traipse all over the West.'

'Sorry,' Lee mumbled. He never knew what to say in situations like that. He noticed Jack approaching them, ready and eager to go on to the next great adventure. Lee turned to Manassas and without raising his eyes as he adjusted his saddle, said, 'The hound can't come along, Calvin.'

'He won't be no trouble, Lee! He never is.'

'Jack can't come. You'll have to tell him to stay. Will he do it?'

'Sure, he will, but Lee . . . it'll break his heart. He won't make no noise.'

'What if he does? What if he gets startled? What if a rabbit runs across his nose and he gives out one little yip?'

Calvin nodded dolefully. He knew that Lee was right. What would poor old Jack think if he was left in the village? Damn all! 'You stay, Jack, hear me? You can't go to war.'

Jack sat, disappointed and unbelieving at first. He went everywhere Manassas went. Always.

'You stay here!'

Calvin swung aboard his pony. Lee and Darby were already mounted, ready to go. Manassas glanced once at the hound and then heeled his pony into motion and they trailed out of the corral. Four Dove had re-emerged from the single women's tent and now she rushed to Lee's side. He reined up sharply as the woman held onto his stirrup.

'So soon?' Four Dove asked, her dark eyes studying Lee's.

'The sooner the better.'

'I will get my pony.'

'You will do no such thing! You will remain here and take care of the white woman. What can she do without you. You at least speak her language and can explain matters.'

'I do not care for the white woman!' Four Dove spat. 'I care for you.'

'Then obey me as you would your father,' Lee said ruggedly. He nodded his head back toward the corral where the dismal yellow hound lay supine, its eyes hopeful. 'You would be no more help than old Jack there.'

She cursed then. Darby did not know the words – they were in the Cheyenne tongue, but he knew them for curses. Lee started Shoshone on at a heedless walk and Four Dove watched the men go, her arms folded beneath her breasts, her eyes as dark and hard as flint.

'You were pretty hard on her, weren't you?' Manassas asked.

'Do you want to be responsible for leading her into battle? I won't have her hurt!' Lee snapped. There was no answer to that, and so they continued on their way in silence, each having left a loved one behind.

The sun cresting the jagged high peaks glittered across the snowfields and blinded them. Each man tugged his hat as low as possible. They made for the darkness of the deep pine forest, finding a trail that even Manassas did not know existed, but then Lee had ridden or walked every foot of his huge parcel over the years – which of course was one card Lee meant to play against the baron and his army.

As they rode, Lee asked Darby Pierce, 'Did they move the wagon where the reloader works, or did they leave it in the little hollow on this side of the creek?'

'I don't know, Lee,' Darby replied. 'The last time I saw it, that's where it was. Why?'

Manassas was also curious, glancing at Lee as they wound through the deep forest where only here and there golden shafts of sunlight poured through the enclosing pines.

'You have something in mind,' Calvin said around his stubby pipe's stem. The pipe was not lit – the scent of tobacco smoke carries too far for it to be safe.

'I have something in mind,' Lee acknowledged. Their horses' hoofs made no sound on the damp pine needles.

'What?' Darby asked with exasperation. Why could Lee not explain his plan?

'What?' Lee repeated. 'Why, Darby, what is in that wagon? A man works there reloading the cartridges the hunting party expends every day – hundreds of them. What with? Gunpowder, a lot of gunpowder. Primers, lead bullets. They can't fight without ammunition, can they?' Lee asked, adding grimly, 'and they tell me that a dozen barrels of powder can make the damnedest explosion you ever will see.'

'It would leave them with nothing except the bullets they have on their belts,' Manassas said, understanding Lee's theory.

'They're sure as hell not riding to the local general store,' Lee said with a touch of humor, 'that being a hundred miles away. Besides,' he commented with quiet irony, 'I've always wondered what fifty pounds of black powder looked like when it was touched off.'

'Good Lord!' Darby Pierce exclaimed. 'It would. . . .'

'Yes, it would,' Lee agreed. 'I might need some help building a new cabin, Manassas. If that gunpowder does what I think it will do.'

'Anybody around. . . .' Pierce said, growing uneasy.

'Yeah,' Lee said fiercely. 'They'd have about as much chance as a grazing wapiti fawn in the sights of a scoped gun. And as much chance as they mean to give Great Elk . . . and us.'

'Still!' Darby Pierce protested, surprised to find that the palms of his hands were sweating.

'This is no time to break out your scruples, Darby. This is a war and they started it. You don't roll over and let yourself be slaughtered just so you don't hurt them.'

Darby Pierce knew that Lee was right, but his upbringing had not prepared him for this sort of frontier morality. He did not like it, but he thought of Great Elk, of Four Dove, of Lucinda! Tragedy could only befall all of these people if the baron prevailed. He steeled himself to the necessity of the moment and trailed silently behind Lee Trent and Manassas.

They rode with infinite patience throughout the day. They could not be discovered by human eyes in the deep forest, Lee believed, but still he rode carefully, his eyes always searching the land before them. Too much depended on wariness. When dusk had again gathered they paused in a deep copse and waited for coming darkness. They did not speak because it was not necessary, and because they did not want their voices to carry to unseen ears.

By the stars it was nearly nine o'clock when they mounted again and approached their goal.

The long valley before Lee's house was alive with activity when the three men, leaving their horses behind, crept near to the forest verge.

Men sat in circles around camp-fires and hoisted cups containing either coffee or something stronger. In Lee's house itself there was a glow of firelight; smoke curled fitfully from the chimney. Voices were raised in loud merriment. Lee frowned as he watched two men exit the cabin, another enter. They had surely made themselves at home.

Further away the wagons rested in a crescent – the wooden armaments wagon, the taxidermist's Conestoga, the supply wagon and, first in line, the one Lee thought to be the reloader's canvas-covered wagon. He whispered into Pierce's ear.

'Is that the one, the one in front?'

'That's where the powder is, yes,' Pierce said in a rather shaky voice.

'Let's pull back,' Lee said jerking a thumb across his shoulders and they rose from their crouches to retreat more deeply into the woods.

'I don't like the layout much, Lee,' Manassas said, from the heavy shadows. The old man continued to bite on the stem of his cold pipe.

'I'm not crazy about it myself. There's too much open ground to traverse before I get to the wagon.'

'You?' Darby Pierce asked. 'Why you?'

'It's my job. It's my home and my war,' Lee said.

'Look,' Pierce asked, as a gust of wind shifted the tops of the tall pines, causing a few cones to drop nearby, 'isn't there a better way than going down there? I mean – could we shoot into the wagon or something?' There was still shakiness in the Easterner's voice. He was afraid. That was all right. Despite his fear he had come along with them. A man had the right to grow a little edgy in the moments before battle.

'Shoot at the powder? That'd never work,' Manassas said with a small chuckle. 'You don't understand, Darby. The gunpowder needs a spark to set it off. Well, an expended bullet won't cause a spark unless it happens to meet metal. You could probably spend the entire magazine of all of our rifles shooting straight into a barrel of gunpowder without causing any more harm than a bunch of wormholes. It'd be like trying to start a camp-fire by firing your pistol into a pile of kindling – as I've actually heard of some fools trying. That might make a lot of noise, but the result would be something less than desired.'

'I'm sorry,' Darby said, removing his hat to run his fingers through his thick blond curls. 'I should have known that. Maybe I did. It was a silly suggestion. I guess, it's just that there's dozens of men down there ready to kill Lee if they spot him.'

'It's full dark,' Lee said.

'And starry-clear,' Darby responded.

'Sometimes there's no choice. When we get past midnight and there's fewer of them abroad, I'll snake my way down the cut and work toward the wagon.'

'No.' Darby was definite. 'Your way is not the

way to go, Lee.'

'You have another idea?' Lee asked.

'Yes,' Darby answered, 'I do.'

'I hope it's better than the last one,' Manassas grumbled.

'It is. Listen,' Darby said intently. 'I'm the one who has to go down there. Isn't that obvious? They know me. I'll make up a story. I'd just say I was searching for Lucinda all day but got myself lost while I was trying it. They'll believe that.'

'The baron wouldn't.'

'Well, maybe he would, maybe not. I should be able to steer clear of the duke and the baron both. They're in your cabin, aren't they.'

'At a guess,' Lee acknowledged.

Darby went on, 'If they do catch me, I'll just continue with my bluff, if they disarm me, well, then it'll be your turn to give it a try, Lee. The cowboys, the trailhands won't know or even be curious about me. It's the only way,' the young man said.

Manassas said after a moment, 'You know he's right, Lee.' He reached for his pipe automatically, and jammed it away again in his pocket. The three crouched in silence, waiting for Lee to speak. Lee, for his part, didn't like the idea. But, he was forced to admit finally, 'Yeah. Darby – you're right. Are you up to it?'

'I don't know,' Darby said honestly. 'I've never

tried anything like this before. Tell me the best way to go about it. We'll find out soon enough if I was up to the job . . . one way or the other.'

Manassas and Lee exchanged an uncertain glance. Neither man responded. In silent agreement then, Calvin searched for and picked up a slab of bone-dry bark and began splintering it with his bowie knife. Darby watched him in some puzzlement.

'What's he doing?' he asked Lee as Calvin took the individual sections of wood he had cut and rubbed them vigorously between his callused palms, reducing them to splinters.

'Tinder,' Lee told the Easterner. 'It'll catch quick and burn hot. The reloader's wagon has a canvas roof. If you can place the tinder on the wagon bed, position it and strike fire, it should catch hold of the canvas quickly.'

'I see, yes,' Darby replied.

'Have you got matches?' Manassas asked, looking up from his work.

'I think so, I. . . .' He began patting his pockets. Manassas could see the man's face silhouetted against the screen of silver stars. Fear lingered in his eyes. To talk about performing a great task and realizing that the time has come to actually accomplish it are vastly different.

'No matter,' Calvin said. 'I've got plenty. I'll not be smoking my pipe tonight.' Or perhaps never again, he thought.

The bundle of tinder Calvin had shredded from the dry bark was given to Darby who tucked it inside his shirt. The blond man swung aboard his horse and then hesitated. Bending down, he asked Lee, 'What if that man – the reloader – is in the wagon?'

'I don't think he'd be fool enough to sleep in there, next to all that powder. If he is inside,' Lee said gravely, 'well – we're in a war and he happens to be on the wrong side.'

'Yes,' Darby muttered. It seemed to be sinking in for the first time that the explosion might kill a man. And, if done properly, perhaps many men.

'Simply ride into camp,' Lee advised. 'Maybe pour yourself a cup of coffee. After awhile saunter across the meadow. There's no reason anyone should stop you. They've all known you for months. Then place the tinder, strike fire. . . .'

'And get the hell out of there as fast as you can,' Manassas told him.

'Make for the creek,' Lee said. 'There should be a lot of confusion, enough to cover your movements in case you happen to be seen setting the fire. Forget your horse. Get to the creek, and, if you can, to the forest beyond.

'Darby,' Lee asked, 'are you really up to this. Because if you're not, I'd rather go myself.'

'I'm up to it,' Darby said through clenched

teeth as if Lee had insulted him, challenged his manhood. He yanked his reins and turned the horse's head around toward the long valley where still the hunting party seemed to be carousing in celebration. To a man they must have been certain that they had found their new home range, a vast and lush country there for the taking. And that they had taken it.

Calvin and Lee stood side by side in the shadows of the tall trees, watching Darby walk his pony slowly downslope.

'I sure hope we done the right thing,' Calvin said quietly. Lee glanced questioningly at the old mountain man. 'Because if we didn't . . .'

'I know,' Lee replied. Because if they had placed their trust in the wrong man, a man they barely knew, they had signed their own death warrant. All Darby Pierce had to do, if he were a sneak and a liar sent to discover their plans was to whisper in one man's ear, let the baron know where Lee and Manassas were hiding and sit back to watch them be ridden down and murdered.

They waited tensely, watching as the man from Baltimore emerged from the dark hem of the forest verge and walked his horse into the camp of the hunters.

EIGHT

Darby Pierce could almost feel their eyes on his back as he trailed his horse across the long grass valley from the pine forest. He knew that Lee Trent and Manassas did not fully trust him. He supposed that this shouldn't make him angry, but it did in a distant way. He had ridden a long way with the duke and Baron Stromberg in order to fulfill his father's promise, to help the old man obtain an Atlantic contract with the Europeans. Then, latterly, he had to admit, he had ridden because of Lucinda. Maybe he could do nothing to protect her, but he had sworn to try. When the Texans had joined their band, Darby had grown even more uneasy about things. John Saturday, for example. How could anybody trust that thin, pale-eyed man. The one they called Pawnee was just as bad, Darby thought, the way he prowled around Lucinda's wagon, the way his eyes trailed her wherever she went.

It was amazing that Duke von Hefflen hadn't noticed it and tried to horsewhip the scarred, powerfully built cowboy – Darby smiled involuntarily. That would have been a fight to see.

He supposed the duke had noticed all of this, the baron as well and had decided their need for these hired guns was more important than poor Lucinda's welfare. Darby also had to suppose that John Saturday had his own private thoughts about keeping this prime land for himself. How could a single one of them trust the others? Darby shook his head. Men living lives of crime would fall in with anyone out of expediency, and each of them always thought he was smarter than the others. Left to themselves, Darby considered, one group would eventually exterminate the other out of sheer greed.

He was not going to let matters go that far. The whole mob was a filthy boil that needed to be lanced. He patted the bundle of tinder beneath his shirt, his surgical tool.

Entering the camp his nerves remained at hair-trigger level. Darby halted his horse, swung down and loosened the cinch on his horse's saddle. He looked around with more concern than he knew he should show, but the night was dark; only the faces of the men sitting around the camp-fires showed plainly, brightened and then darkened by shifting flame and smoke.

He passed a Bavarian he knew only slightly and nodded without speaking. A moment later he passed two Texans, their drawls thickened by whiskey. He continue on his way, his legs trembling slightly, his heart pounding. The pulse in his head sounded in the depths of his ears like a locomotive's drive wheels.

He passed Lucinda's empty wagon and then the supply Conestoga. His throat was constricted now. His left hand was clenched around the tinder, his right hovered over his holstered pistol like an uncertain spider. He could see the dark form of the reloader's wagon now, its canvas top pale against the backdrop of starlit sky, broad meadow and the serrated ranks of pine trees beyond the creek.

'Where in hell do you think you're going?' a voice challenged from out of the night and Darby froze as the Texas gunhand approached him, his big Colt Navy revolver cocked and leveled.

'For a walk, what's the matter with you!' Darby shot back, managing to inject some authority into his voice.

'Oh, it's you, sir. Sorry,' the Texan said, holstering his pistol. 'We were told to keep a sharp eye out tonight, you see?'

'It's all right,' Darby said, feeling relief flow back into his tense body. 'I just wanted to have a look around myself. Never know who's prowling about. Not with the Indians so close.'

'You're right there,' the cowboy said, rubbing his whiskered chin. 'I don't like this much.'

'It'll soon be over,' Darby promised.

'I hope so. Well, good night.'

'Good night,' Darby said as the man ambled off. His legs still hadn't stopped trembling. Breathing a small, potent curse, he continued on his way.

There was not a close sound in the night except for the quiet flow of the creek over stones. Distantly – from time to time – a man yelled with delight or cursed. Ahead the wagon rested as silent as a sepulchre. Darby slipped beside it, glanced both ways and with shaking hands jammed the tinder between the side of the wagon bed and the heavy canvas top. He looked around again at the silent night, took a deep breath and lit a match. The head broke from it and a small sulphurous bead of flame fell to the grass. Cursing softly, he tried again. The second match caught fire cleanly and he let the flame kiss the tinder.

The canvas caught almost immediately, a widening black hole forming behind a rapidly rising ring of flame. Someone yelled out, 'Hey! What's going on back there.' Then, 'Fire!'

The silhouette of a man, his rifle lowered,

appeared from around the corner of the wagon and without forethought, without anger or fear, Darby shot him dead. The man flung out one arm and fell to the dark grass of the meadow. There was a second, more distant yell and Darby Pierce took to his heels, running blindly across the valley toward the silver stream as the fire leaped and twisted with savage quickness along the canvas back of the wagon.

There was chaos behind him although Darby did not pause to watch it. Some men rushed toward the flames with blankets, others, recognizing the danger of explosion, yipped and ran as fast as their legs would allow, in the opposite direction. Horses reared up and whinnied in panic. The baron, Duke von Hefflen and their helmeted bodyguards emerged from Lee's cabin and filled the air with unintelligible curses and conflicting commands.

The Texans continued to retreat, but the baron's more disciplined soldiers, used to obeying without question rushed toward the burning wagon with water buckets and smouldering blankets.

When the flames touched the gunpowder the roar of the explosion shook the ground and hurled half-a-dozen men skyward. Lee Trent didn't wait for the smoke to clear before he began deliberately shooting at the scattered men below. He caught the first man in his sights and shot him as emotionlessly as a target in a shooting gallery. Manassas, prone on the ground beside him, touched off a round and Lee saw a second intruder go down. A second explosion rattled the night and Lee ducked his head, covering up with his hat, letting the flash subside before he lifted his eyes again. Three or four men, their vision temporarily lost to the fierce red and yellow explosion had drawn their guns to fight, but there was no visible enemy. They let loose a barrage of shots, and in the confusion it was a miracle if some of them didn't kill or wound their own people.

'Idiots,' Lee heard Manassas mutter. Then the old mountain man cocked his rifle and shot one of the uniformed Prussians from his horse as the man tried to flee the confusion. The background graduated from brilliant crimson at ground level to shimmering gold to total blackness above where the roiling smoke rose against a purpled sky. It was hell below, but it was perfect for a sniper – dark silhouettes stood out distinctly against the flare and flame of the fire.

The wagon which had been blown into the air to land on its side now began to turn to charred wood. By the dimming firelight they could see men scattered across the meadow from the force of the explosion. Smoke still billowed skyward, but the light for shooting had gone. Even the fireplace glow in Lee's cabin had gone, extinguished no doubt from within. There were no remaining targets but shadows and smoke.

'We got to go hunting now, Lee,' Manassas said.

They recovered their horses, carefully checked the loads in their weapons and started down, not in a wild charge, but in a carefully conceived foray against the enemy who still held their land, and if given the chance to regroup, might hold it.

Darby Pierce had run toward the creek in blind haste as the wagon top had flared up and the following explosion had racketed across the valley. He hit the icy water of the stream at a full run and fell almost immediately, his boots finding no purchase against the slick river-bottom stones. Falling headlong, he rose again and rushed on as behind him another roar of exploding gunpowder sounded. The creek was knee-deep at midstream and his movements seemed terrifyingly slow as he tried to raise his sodden legs and boots, to escape somehow from the gunfire which now creased the night silence violently. He half-crawled up the opposite bank through mud and long grass.

Lying on his belly he rolled his head back toward the firelit scene, seeing men die, loose

133

wild shots, horses stampede in panic. He knew that Lee and Manassas were firing from the hillside because unexpectedly a man would collapse on his face never to rise and others dashed toward the woods beyond the house, strange, wildly-excited silhouettes against the gold and crimson of the night.

Darby rose to a sitting position, his head hanging, his clothing soaked through with mud, his body trembling with the cold.

He felt like a coward suddenly, although he had done his work. He should be over there, joined in the fighting, but he hadn't the energy or the heart for it just then. He sat with his filthy hair pasted across his forehead, staring numbly at the hell he had sparked.

Lee Trent turned Shoshone toward the house. The sporadic, ill-aimed gunfire did not startle the mountain horse. The red roan was used to hunting and gunfire, although this was on a vastly greater scale. Manassas had turned aside some little way back, but Lee had paid scant attention. He knew where the duke and Baron Stromberg were. They had tried to take his land and now they had taken his home for their own. In his heart was a feeling as disgusted and yet as determined as if he had come home from abroad to find his house infested with rats. These men were killers. They wanted him dead, they wanted the Cheyenne dead, they gave no thought at all to the slaughtering of hundreds of fine, magnificent animals.

Very well – they deserved no pity themselves.

A guard's bright helmet reflected firelight from the smoldering wagon as he rose up and shouldered his rifle. Without hesitation Lee shot him down, his spinning .44 slug going neatly through the helmet and the man died, far away from his homeland and loved ones.

Ducking low over Shoshone's withers, he spurred the big roan on. Two startled Texans spun and fired rapidly at him. Lee shot the first one and rode Shoshone directly over the second. The door to the cabin opened and someone from within fired a near shot at Lee. He put two bullets through the door in return and swung down from Shoshone on the run, diving into deeper shadows beneath the oaks beside the chimney.

He had hit the ground hard, and as he rolled into the shelter of the dark trees, he felt sharp pain in his lower ribcage. He growled a silent curse, hoping he had not broken one or more, knowing he most probably had. He was still for a moment, listening to the scattered gunfire, the occasional flitting shadow. Then he rose to his feet and moved nearer to the house.

Lee kept below the only window on that side of

the cabin and moved to the corner of the house. His face was bathed in sweat now, his gun hand slick. He holstered his pistol and dug in his pockets. It was the night of fire, and it had not ended yet. Lee scraped together a pile of pine needles and twigs from the surrounding oaks and built a tiny pyre. He hated to burn the house – it had taken him a summer to build.

Yet there were only a few ways to rid yourself of rats, and this one would drive the vermin from their hiding place. He struck a match and watched as his tinderbox started to smoke to life and then catch fiery life. Holding his broken ribs, he raced back into the oaks and worked his way back to where he had a view of the front of the house. He waited, and it was not long before the squared timbers of the log cabin began to glow and then ignite and hot flames to lick at the sides of the cabin. When they reached the eaves, the cabin exploded with fire.

I've got to remember to fix that next time, maybe haul some slate in, Lee thought as he levered a round into the chamber of his Winchester and waited. He had set fire to his own house, and it was a miserable feeling to watch it send fountains of golden sparks into the cold night. But then he had lived upon this land before he had had a shelter of any kind. There was still the small cabin. . . .

A uniformed man came running out onto the porch from the smoke-filled cabin, firing in every direction but the one Lee held. Grimly he sighted the Winchester repeater and fired a single clean shot through the soldier's heart.

He could imagine the turmoil and panic inside the cabin as it filled with smoke and the flames began to build. How would they come out – one by one, each man taking his chance, or in a mob, firing every direction at once? No matter – Lee would be able to see each of them clearly; they would have to locate his muzzle flash, no easy feat with firelight in their eyes. He waited, drawing back the hammer on the rifle once more.

Calvin Manassas saw the flames start at the rear of the cabin and he chuckled. Lee was going to get those men out of there, and his house be damned. Calvin himself had dismounted and had slithered up into the mound of yellow boulders at the south end of the encampment. The trail south, he figured, was going to become a very popular road shortly. The men in the valley could not possibly tell in the darkness what they were facing. For all they knew there was a war party of Cheyenne surrounding them, waiting to take their scalps. No sooner had Manassas considered that than a Texas cowboy, riding hell for leather bolted toward him on a paint pony, flagging the wide-eyed horse with his hat.

Manassas let the rider approach nearer. Then just as he passed the boulders, Calvin raised up and fired a shot. He hadn't aimed at the cowhand who obviously had no interest in the fight any longer, only getting started back toward the Panhandle as soon as possible, but the slug from Calvin's Winchester burned the paint pony's flank and it lifted into a headlong gallop which the Texan couldn't have slowed if he had wished to.

'Manassas,' a voice whispered roughly from the shadows, and Calvin, cursing himself for playing games when he should have been serious as death, whirled and went to his back, ready to fire from that awkward position.

'God's sake, don't shoot! It's me!'

A man who looked as if he had been dipped in mud and then dusted with bog-float lifted both hands and then crept forward at a duckwalk. Darby Pierce sat down in a weary collapse.

'Damn it,' Manassas hissed, 'I almost shot you.'

'I know it,' Darby said through chattering teeth.

'You were supposed to be long gone across the creek.'

'I came back. I couldn't run out on you two.'

Calvin nodded silently and then told him, 'Check your loads, son, it's going to be a long night still.'

'I saw a bunch of them riding off,' Darby said as he checked his Colt's barrel for mud and debris. 'Does that mean it's nearly over?'

Calvin shook his head. 'Those boys were riding for pay and a promise of an easy life on the Wapiti Trail. They weren't up to this. The foreigners, now,' Manassas said nodding toward the meadow, 'they're a long way from home with nowhere to go. They swore loyalty to the baron, I reckon. They're plenty afraid, but they have no option but to keep on.

'Let's see how good they are at Indian fighting.'

Lee Trent heard a few evenly-spaced shots to the south near the clump of boulders and then a dozen or more. He saw no one among the soldiers shooting back. Possibly they could find no target. If that was Manassas, he'd be dug into the boulders good and proper and all they would be able to do against him in the darkness was to splinter some rocks and deplete their ammunition which now could not be replenished, with their armory wagon destroyed.

The fire in the cabin continued to burn hotly, vermilion and golden flames licking against the underbelly of the night. They would have to come out soon or be roasted alive. He waited, whistling tunelessly, the Winchester cool in his hands. Somewhere in the corner of his mind, far away, he apologized to Ulysses. I should never have let them take you.

The first man appeared in the frame of the flung-open cabin door. He dove across the porch and hit the ground rolling, gun in his hand. Lee sighed inwardly, drew evenly back on the trigger of his repeating rifle and shot the man. Two others had been in the doorway trying to elbow each other out of the way. Now they fought each other just as wildly, trying to get back inside.

Lee heard footsteps behind him above the uproar and realized the man he had shot had been a sacrificial lamb. There was someone in the oaks now. He must have slithered out the tiny window on the other side of the cabin to discover Lee's position when he fired. Now Lee rolled to one side just as a gun exploded at near quarters and he fired back at the shadowed figure. The man screamed and threw his hands over his face.

Lee rolled back but it was too late. Half-a-dozen men had broken from the cabin and they leveled their fire in his direction. He was forced to scramble behind the trunk of a huge oak and his next two shots tagged nothing as the band of men dispersed in the night. From the pile of boulders to the south Lee heard two guns firing at the escaping men, but he doubted Manassas had hit any of them either.

Two guns? Had Darby somehow managed to

rejoin the fight?

A Texan, hatless, aboard a chestnut horse at full gallop rode directly past Lee and was gone before Lee could lever another round in to the receiver of his Winchester and throw his sights on him. How many had run? How many were dead or injured? There was no telling.

Lee withdrew a little way into the oak grove and then circled toward the back of the house, slipping through the pines toward the north to continue the fight. He had not seen the duke or Baron Stromberg among the fleeing men, but if they were not out of the house by now, they would never rejoin the conflict, for the cabin fire had flared up with awesome swiftness, and curling flames twisting together as if in battle for dominance crackled and roared. The cabin could not last another ten minutes. Lee moved on through the pines, his mouth set grimly as he continued on through the savage night.

NINE

Manassas was worried. He and Darby were doing the best they could, but their position was a defensive one. Sooner or later the enemy would begin to surround them on all sides. Behind them the forest, too near for comfort, covered any movements.

'We've got to take it to them,' Calvin said. 'Besides, Lee is out there alone now.'

Darby didn't answer. He wiped his forehead with the back of his wrist and it came away filthy with mud and a streak of crimson blood from some wound he didn't remember getting. He understood Manassas well enough. They could only remain in the same position for so long before the intruders closed in on them.

'Let the cabin fire burn itself out,' Calvin said. 'Then when the darkness settles again, we'll move. Whyn't you try to get into the pines and work north. I'm going to head for the creek and try to shelter behind the banks.'

'As you say,' Darby said in a voice breathless with the excitement. He patted his pockets and told Manassas, 'I'm down to ten rounds or less.'

'I've got half a box of spares. I'll split 'em with you.' Calvin said, taking twenty-five brass cartridges from the cardboard box in his jacket pocket. A few shells scattered across the rocks and disappeared down crevices. Calvin cursed and held out a cupped handful of shells to Darby who dropped two bullets himself as he kept his eyes focused on the surrounding land. The fire in the cabin had nearly burned itself out, but by its imperfect light he had counted nearly a dozen dead men scattered across the meadow.

Shakily he pocketed the extra cartridges. 'I hope they're as low on ammunition as we are. When do we go?' he asked Manassas in a trembling voice. He had no wish to expose himself to enemy fire.

'The smoke's drifting low,' Manassas said, 'we got a better chance now than we ever will.'

Having said that Manassas nodded goodbye to the young man and slithered back down the boulders, hit the ground hard and ran toward the riverbank. No shots followed him, nor did any shots ring out when Darby slid down the rocks and raced toward the shelter of the pines. Black smoke still drifted across the valley like war smoke after a cannon volley.

Manassas lost sight of Darby within a few yards. Besides, it was no time to look after Pierce. Running in a low crouch, Calvin ran on toward the creek, his rifle at the ready. He hit the soft ground at the stream's edge and slipped more than slid down the bank to the water's edge. He heard three shots from the north and hoped they were Lee's, hoped they had done their cause some good.

There was another sudden spate of shots behind him, but no lead sang past Manassas. He figured the enemy had opened up on the stack of boulders, hoping their wild shots might drive the Elk Range men out.

Still moving in a low crouch, his breath coming more roughly, the old mountain man followed the river northward. He tripped over an unseen rock and his rifle clattered free. Scrambling to recover it he heard a chilling voice directly behind him.

'Kind of clumsy, aren't you, old-timer?' A victorious laugh followed and Calvin turned his head enough to see the scarred, muscular Texan they called Pawnee standing nearly over him with his Colt revolver cocked and leveled. The rifle was inches from Calvin's hand, but it may as well have been miles.

'Well, you had a long enough run, old man,' Pawnee said, leveling the barrel of his pistol at Calvin. Then Manassas saw a blur of movement, a yellow-black flash of shadow and the Texan, half turning, suddenly threw his arms into the air and screamed as Calvin leaped for his rifle. 'My leg's torn open!' Pawnee bellowed.

Calvin took one step back and fired two shots directly into the Texan's body. Then he sagged to the muddy earth, his heart driving in heavy thuds against his ribs.

'Didn't I tell you to *stay*!' Calvin said with nervous excitement and Jack laid his big yellow head on Calvin's leg while the mountain man rubbed the hound's head in grateful admiration. 'Why don't you do what you're told, Jack? . . . and thank God you didn't.' Calvin rose on unsteady legs and stared down at Pawnee for a moment. Then he said, 'Let's get moving, Jack. Someone might be coming.'

Lee Trent moved silently through the shadows spread over the battlefield. The dead littered the ground, some of them blackened, their clothing still smoking from the explosion. He had seen other men on the move. A few of them – mostly the Texas cowhands – riding as fast as they could from the valley, not even looking back. Others he had seen slipping into the forest to regroup and make some sort of desperate plan.

He had let them all go unless he was directly challenged. He had no time to fight the pawns wandering across the chessboard whose defense had crumbled. He wanted the knight and the king – he was sure there was no bishop among the men standing.

The night had grown cool; the stars were as bright as ever but they appeared like dots of ice against the blue-black of the sky. He heard no animals stirring, no sounds of the hunting night-birds. They wanted no part of this deadly man-game.

Lee halted in his tracks, crouched, the big blue Colt revolver cold and comforting in his hand. He had discarded the Winchester. It was close-in work that now needed to be done, and he hadn't enough ammunition for both weapons.

Frowning, he remained fixed in position. Something had caught his eye, a fleeting shadow, but he could not fix it in his mind. Then he saw it again, more distinct now. A man inside the taxidermist's wagon with all its grisly trophies had made an ill-conceived move. He had raised the curtain behind the small side window a mere inch or so to peer out. Lee, motionless, had not caught the man's eye. The curtain lowered again and Lee rushed on feet as silent as a hunting cougar's.

He had found the king, he was certain. In that

one brief glimpse he had recognized Baron Stromberg. Lee's mouth tightened with disgust. The man had hidden himself away like a weasel while other men shed their blood for him.

Lee drew up beside the wagon's front wheel, letting his heartbeat slow. He breathed the cold air deeply and waited and briefly looked to the far peaks with their magnificent shoulders clad in eternal snow. A boot trod ever so gently on the floorboards inside the wagon, but its faint squeak as the boards moved was obvious.

Lee smiled without a shadow of humor and began working his way toward the rear of the wagon, his pistol held, barrel up, beside his ear. He crouched as he reached the rear of the wagon. The wooden steps leading up to the wagon were down, but the door was closed and undoubtedly locked or barricaded. Around him was only the silence of the night. Nothing moved, no man cried out an alarm.

There was no way into the wagon but through the wooden door.

There was no other way out of it either.

The baron was a rifleman, but was he practiced at close fighting with handguns? Lee doubted it, but then you never knew. It was folly to try it alone, foolish to rush the door, but then perhaps there were other soldiers out there, unseen, ready to gather if he waited too long to make his move.

Lee tried it.

He mounted the steps as softly as an Indian in moccasins. Then, with his chest rising and falling heavily, he leaned as far away from the door as possible and rapped on it with the barrel of his gun. There was an immediate, explosive reaction. The blast of an incredibly powerful rifle being triggered off slammed a bullet through the door, forming a rosette of splinters inches from Lee's eyes.

He didn't give the rifleman a chance to reload. Lee drew back and drove his shoulder against the heavy door and it fell inward on weak and rusted hinges. Baron Stromberg was there among his wealth of trophies, drawn back against the far wall where the bear paws dangled like decorations on a huge grisly garland.

He was frantically trying to reload his rifle. His eyes goggled at Lee as he fumbled one massive cartridge after another to the floor of the wagon. His clothing was torn and fire-smudged, his mustache, formerly immaculately groomed was a sodden silver ruff across his mouth.

Finding some last remnant of angry pride, Stromberg switched his hands to the barrel of the rifle and swung it with all of his strength at Lee's head. The attempt missed wildly as the rifle ended its half circle against the wagon's wall, breaking the stock.

Lee could have shot and killed the baron easily at that moment, but he discovered a secret ember glowing in his heart. A vengeful ember that urged him not to kill the baron simply with a twitch of his finger, but to beat him into insensibility with his fists.

Lee leaped toward the panicked man and swung a crushing right hand to the baron's temple. For a moment they grappled, the baron showing unsuspected strength in his thick body. He was many things, the baron, but not a hand-to-hand fighter. Lee jabbed him twice with his left fist. The second blow splintered the baron's nose, spattering both of them with blood. Lee followed with a right hand, this one landing with all the strength of his powerful shoulders on the hinge of the European's jaw.

Baron Stromberg was beaten, but he did not quit. He staggered backward, jolted badly by the onslaught of Lee's fists, but remained upright. They grappled again, rolling onto a pile of hides and bearskins and then hit the bare wooden floor, both men flailing wildly. The baron rose, stumbled back into a row of deer and pronghorn antelope antlers, bringing them down from the wall to litter the floor with their bony barbs.

He tried to attack Lee but the baron had exceeded his physical resources now, and his swinging fists seemed pudgy and his blows ineffective. Each time he missed, Lee's left, jolting like the butt of a sawn log, landed against the baron's face. It was now a mottled, disfigured mass of raw flesh. Blood leaked from his broken nose and from his ears. One eye was nearly closed and his lower lip was split. For another man Lee would have shown mercy, knowing he had beaten his adversary, but the heat from the tiny ember still burned hotly.

From a table in the corner of the wagon, the baron swept up something small, bright and savage. Lee knew it for what it was – the taxidermist's skinning knife, sharp as a razor and much more deadly. The baron's eyes glowed with killing fervor as he hefted it, holding it low beside his hip.

'You have hurt me too much,' Stromberg whispered hoarsely. 'You have ruined everything. All my plans for a new life.'

'What was the matter with your old one?' Lee asked as they warily circled. 'They couldn't stomach a man like you in your own country either? Isn't that so!'

'There were pigs there as well,' the baron said. 'I killed two of them, like I will butcher you now, Lee Trent.'

He lunged then with the knife aimed at Lee's stomach. Lee turned just enough to slap the knife slightly aside as he twisted away from the blade.

Simultaneously he managed to backheel the onrushing baron. His heel struck behind Stromberg's ankle and the baron lost his footing. He flew backward, his eyes angry and deadly.

His body fell heavily and Lee stood back, waiting for his next move.

There was none.

As Lee watched, panting with the exertion, his fists still doubled tightly, the hate, the deadly intent went out of the baron's eyes. He opened his hand and the knife dropped from his fingers to clatter against the wagon-bed. Lee frowned, not understanding for a long minute. Then, moving nearer, he saw what had happened.

The baron was dead. Through his chest a dagger-like row of frozen bone sprouted like the angry fangs of retribution. And beneath him lay the severed trophy rack of antlers slashed from the skull of Ulysses. Lee turned shakily toward the door of the wagon.

He moved out into the cool night and slumped to seat himself on the wagon's second step, rubbing at his throbbing temples with his thumbs.

'Ever it is so,' a voice said from the darkness. 'Defeat must always follow victory.'

Lee lifted his eyes to fmd Duke von Hefflen, his white shirt unbuttoned, standing before him, rifle positioned.

'The baron – poor man,' the duke said mockingly as he studied the dead man. 'He thought he would gain an easy victory over a few rough mountain men, and a handful of Indians he could remove with the help of your own government! Of course,' von Hefflen admitted, 'I would eventually have removed the pompous fool myself. Murder is so simple out here, is it not?

'But you have done that for me. Do you understand what I have said to you? You see, Trent, you too, believed only seconds ago that you had won a victory. Now here I am to bring the inevitable. You have become the defeated!'

He raised the rifle, shouldered it and sighted. But his finger never tightened on the curved trigger. Instead a whisper of sound darted across the meadow and the duke dropped his weapon, throwing confused hands to his throat where an arrow had pierced it from side to side.

Trent leaped to his feet, his legs rubbery, his throat dry. He watched as the duke jerked convulsively three times and collapsed to the bloody earth as Four Dove emerged from the shadows with her bow in her hands and a quiver of arrows on her back. She looked down at the man and nodded with satisfaction. Then her eyes, black and expressionless except for the determination he saw there, went to where Lee stood waiting.

'Damnit!' Lee said, with intermingled emotions, 'didn't I tell you to stay in the village? To obey me as if I were your father.'

She shrugged and said without a smile, 'This is the way I obey my father, Lee. Ask him if that is not so. I brought the old dog and we followed after. He follows sign better in the darkness than I. And so I am here.'

'I asked you not to come!'

'But I came,' Four Dove said blithely.

'And so. . . .'

'And so I am not a good daughter,' she shrugged. 'But I will be a good wife, Lee – for you see, I will fight for my man.'

'You could have been killed,' he said, with a sternness he did not feel.

'And if I had not come you most certainly would be dead right now.' Four Dove bowed her head ever so slightly but not obsequiously. 'From now on, I promise that I will obey you, my husband.'

That seemed most unlikely, but he could not be angry with her. He wasn't so sure as he once had been that it mattered. He was sure of one thing, however.

He had come to love her very much. And – yes, she would be his wife if she was not already.

They started arm in arm across the battlefield. Lee said, 'You should not have left Lucinda alone

153

in the village. What if something had happened to you?'

'I did not leave her, Lee Trent. She cannot fight; no one has ever taught her how, so I left her in the small cabin and told her to wait. Is her man all right?'

'Her man?'

'Darby Pierce. We talked much in the women's tent.' Four Dove nodded definitely. 'He is her man. She talked of nothing else.'

'I haven't seen Darby . . . or Manassas,' Lee had to tell her.

'We will find him,' Four Dove said with expansive optimism. 'He will be all right – and old Manassas. This is a night when the stars hold all of their luck for us.'

Lee could only hope so. He continued to scan the smoky shadows, the forest verge for enemies that might be hiding, waiting.

Disconsolately, he glanced at the remains of his house, nothing but a sad pile of scorched timber and ashes. 'Later,' he told Four Dove as they paused facing each other again, 'I will come to visit your father . . . when I have rebuilt my house.'

'There is the little cabin still,' Four Dove said, waving an impatient hand, 'it is shelter enough. You forget, Lee, that I have slept in the snow beneath nothing more than a buffalo robe. I am

Cheyenne. I need little. Besides, you do not need to speak to my father. I have already told him that we are married and that was that.'

'Without wedding gifts, without horses for your bridal price. Without. . . ?'

'I have already told Great Elk,' Four Dove repeated in her casual, wilful way. 'My father needs no more horses, anyway.'

They had come to the edge of the deep pine forest, continuing to walk arm in arm up the secret path to where the little cabin rested and Lucinda must be waiting anxiously for some word. 'How did he react . . . when you told him?' Lee asked. 'Was he angry?'

'Of course!' Four Dove answered. 'There are rules, laws our people live by. There should have been a bargaining time, festivals.'

'So he was angry?'

'He was angry, Lee, but only on top, you understand?'

'On the surface, you mean?'

'On that,' Four Dove said with a small, nearly sly smile. 'But he was also very happy. He loves me, Lee, and he loves you. He is happy that we will be together. He knows we are meant to be with each other – and to bring him little laughing babies.'

The voice from the pines said, 'That's the most touching thing I've listened to in a long while.

Now put your hands up, Trent.'

John Saturday stepped out into the path and his teeth showed white as he grinned and raised his revolver.

TEN

Lee stood stock still, but he did not hoist his hands as the Texan had ordered him to do. His left hand hung free; his right hovered over the holster where his Colt .44 nestled.

'I said, "raise 'em" Trent!'

'No,' Lee replied softly. The night was unfocused behind the shadows, silent and empty but crowded with the whispers of passing souls. 'I don't believe I will, Saturday. You'll have to shoot it out with me. I've come too far to surrender now.'

The grin the self-styled gunman had worn faded to a frown. This was not the way he had planned things to work out. 'It's not worth your life,' Saturday said, meaning the mountains, the long-grass valley, the quick-flowing silver creek.

'It is to me,' Lee said.

Four Dove seized the moment; there was only a whispery savage sound as she drew an arrow from her quiver and notched the arrow. Saturday twitched and his frown deepened. Lee put a hand on Four Dove's wrist, restraining her. Her eyes were dark fire.

'It is worth it to me as well,' Four Dove told the Texan. 'I will fight for my man – you must know that by now.'

There was a sharp ratcheting sound near at hand and Lee shifted his eyes slightly to watch Manassas emerge from the trees, his rifle in his hands, cocked and ready. 'I think you ought to be asking yourself if it's worth it to you, Saturday,' the old man said.

Saturday looked around uncertainly. His hand still held his pistol, but his grip was looser now. He looked from one man to the other and then to Four Dove, realizing suddenly that he had no chance at all against these three.

'Hell,' he said bitterly. Angrily but smoothly, he holstered his pistol. 'I guess there's nothing left for me, is there?'

'Nothing good,' Lee answered. 'Where's your horse?'

'Over there,' John Saturday answered, inclining his head.

'See if it remembers how to travel,' Lee suggested coldly. 'And if there's any of your bunch around that you know of, invite them along.'

Saturday began to say something, but clamped his jaw shut again. With a short shrug he turned his back to them and walked a little way into the forest. They waited until they could hear the creak of leather as he swung aboard his horse and hear the slow clopping of the animal making its way out of the trees.

When Saturday had reached the meadow and lifted his horse into an easy lope, never once looking back at them, they put their weapons away. Manassas grinned with relief.

'I thought for one moment he was going to try it. I guess there's a reason we never heard of the famous John Saturday, gunman. Hell, he's nothing but another crazy cowboy with a gun.'

Manassas shook his head and stared out across the carnage and destruction in the valley. 'Lee, we've got a hell of a lot of cleaning up to do.'

'Me,' Lee answered, 'not you.'

'Sure me!' Manassas objected.

'No. It's best if you take your wagon down to Rock Springs for your winter supplies before the weather turns.' He added, 'You can take Darby and Lucinda with you and get them started on their way to wherever it is they choose to be.'

'I guess that is the best plan, Lee,' Manassas said as the three of them walked slowly along the winding path to the little cabin, 'But it may be they won't wish to be traveling together.'

159

'I think they will,' Lee said with a grin, because there on the porch of the little cabin, backlighted by a low-burning fire, they saw Lucinda with her arms around Darby Pierce, her head against his chest as he hugged her tightly, his eyes closed and at peace.

'And so, and so,' Four Dove said with humor. 'Lee, my husband, do you think we could give up the cabin to them for one night? You and I can sleep beneath the stars and the long sky.'

'I can't think of a reason in the world not to do that, Four Dove, my wife.' His expression did not change, but his heart held a smile large enough to contain the entire width and breadth of all of the Wapiti Range.